"You weren't entertaining the thought of taking up where you left off last night, by any chance?"

"No!" The denial exploded from him. The fact that that thought had been in his mind made Francesca's accusation that much more damning to him.

"Well, don't let me keep you. You must want to get ready for your date. I'm sure she'll be more receptive than me."

"More grateful, at least," Will snapped. "May I remind you I didn't invite you here?"

Francesca seemed to soften. "I know," she said, looking a little unhappy now.

Will's body tensed. What did she think he was made of? Already his mind was beyond the point of stripping those sexy garments from her. He groped for the door and wrenched it open, wondering how in God's name he was going to let Francesca go....

ANNE MATHER began writing when she was a child, progressing through torrid teenage romances to the kind of adult romances she likes to read. She's married, with two children, and lives in the north of England. After writing, she enjoys reading, driving and traveling to different places to find settings for new novels. She considers herself very lucky to do something that she not only enjoys but also gets paid for.

Books by Anne Mather

HARLEQUIN PRESENTS
1869—WICKED CAPRICE
1887—LONG NIGHT'S LOVING
1911—SHATTERED ILLUSIONS

Also available in MIRA® Books

DANGEROUS TEMPTATION

Anne Mather

Dishonourable Intent

Harlequin Books

TORONTO • NEW YORK • LONDON
AMSTERDAM • PARIS • SYDNEY • HAMBURG
STOCKHOLM • ATHENS • TOKYO • MILAN
MADRID • WARSAW • BUDAPEST • AUCKLAND

ISBN 0-373-11947-X

DISHONOURABLE INTENT

First North American Publication 1998.

Printed in U.S.A.

CHAPTER ONE

HE STOOD at the long mullioned windows of the library,
watching the desultory stream of visitors making their
way towards the exit. He couldn't hear what they were
saying, of course, but their reluctance to leave seemed
evident enough. And, after all, the garden and grounds
of Lingard Abbey were fast becoming one of the most
popular tourist attractions in Yorkshire, the steady influx
of cash the visitors provided slowly enabling him to restore the surroundings of the old house to their former
glory.

At least he could now pay the gardeners a living wage,
he thought wryly, raising one narrow hand to rest it
against the scarred frame. At this time of the year, particularly, the terraces and water gardens were a riot of
colour; even the lake, glittering in the rays of the low-
ering sun, reflected the colours of the trees and shrubs
that surrounded it.

Of course, it would take more than the income from
an unspecified number of tourists to make any serious
assault on the house. Dampness, crumbling stonework,
and the tendency to shriek like a banshee when the wind
invaded the cracks in the woodwork, had made parts of
the Abbey virtually uninhabitable. Which was why he
was considering his grandmother's suggestion that he get
married again. A wealthy wife, who wouldn't demand
too much from him beyond his title, and the only way
he could hope to retain his home.

He scowled, and turned away from the window. It was
archaic, he thought irritably. Imagine marrying someone
in this day and age simply to restore the family fortunes.
It was all very well for his grandmother to declare that

5

it had been an accepted practice when she was young. It was nearly the start of the new millennium, for God's sake! If he did marry again, it ought to be to someone he cared about, at least.

Yet... His scowl deepened. Marrying someone he had cared about hadn't worked before, so why should he assume it would work now? He'd been crazy about Francesca, and she'd walked all over him. Was he really in the market to make that same mistake again?

The answer was a resounding *no*. Even the thought of embarking on another disastrous relationship caused a bitter churning in his gut. Perhaps his grandmother was right; perhaps it was better to be the one who was loved rather than the other way about. He'd loved Francesca, and suffered all the pains of hell when it was over...

A tentative tap on the heavy panels of the door halted his morbid introspection. 'Come in,' he called brusquely, pausing on the worn rug that lay before the impressive hearth, and moments later the angular figure of Watkins, the elderly butler, appeared in the aperture.

'Good evening, my lord,' Watkins greeted him politely. 'Um—Mrs Harvey was wondering if you'd be in to supper,' he explained, with a diffident air. 'And O'Brien asked me to inform you that a pair of electric shears are missing. He left them in the knot garden, but they were not there when he went to fetch them.'

His employer's lips thinned. 'What the hell was O'Brien thinking of, leaving the shears unattended in the first place?' he demanded, and then stifled any further comment at the troubled look on Watkins' face. 'Oh, never mind,' he muttered. 'I'll speak to O'Brien myself in the morning. And, no, I won't be in for supper. I'm dining with Lady Rosemary at Mulberry Court.'

'Yes, my lord.' Watkins glanced hopefully about him. 'Can I get you a drink before I leave?'

'That won't be necessary.' The younger man managed a civil rejoinder. 'Thank you, Watkins. I shan't be needing anything else tonight.'

'No, my lord.' Watkins backed somewhat unevenly towards the door, and, alone again, he reflected that the old man really ought to be retired. He had to be seventy, if he was a day, and had worked for the family since he was a boy. But without his job at the Abbey it was difficult to think how Watkins would survive.

A huge mahogany desk occupied a central position by the windows, and, flinging himself into the worn leather chair behind it, he stared somewhat broodingly into space. Here he was, William Henry Robert Gervaise Quentin, 9th Earl of Lingard, and he couldn't even afford to give his staff a decent pension.

An hour later, bathed and shaved, and with his too long dark hair brushed smoothly behind his ears, he drove the short distance between Lingard Abbey and his grandmother's country home at Mulberry Court. He was trying hard to feel more optimistic, but the thought of the evening ahead was putting a definite strain on his temper. It was all very well to acknowledge his limitations in the comparative anonymity of the Abbey, and quite another to consider the alternative with his grandmother's matchmaking in prospect.

Mulberry Court glowed in the amber light of the summer evening. An attractive manor house, with its origins dating from the sixteenth century, the house and its extensive grounds had been entailed upon his aunt's eldest son. Unfortunately, his cousin Edward had died of leukaemia when he was in his teens, and in consequence the entail was now endowed upon a distant relative of his late grandfather.

It had always been a source of great disappointment to Lady Rosemary that her favourite grandchild was not in line to inherit the estate. The monies devolved from the properties and the like would have enabled him to restore the Abbey without having to resort to a form of legal prostitution, and the old lady did everything in her power to make his life less fraught.

Except when it came to marriage, and the provision

of the next Earl of Lingard, he reflected wryly as he parked his estate car to the right of the front door. In Lady Rosemary's opinion, nothing could compensate for the lack of a wife and family, and she was hopeful that with the right woman he could achieve both ends in one.

A housemaid opened the door at his approach, and he guessed his grandmother had been watching for him. She and her guests were enjoying pre-supper drinks in the orangery, and the pleasant scent of citrus was in the air.

'Will!' His grandmother came to meet him as he halted in the doorway, reaching up to brush dry, papery lips across his newly shaved cheek. 'My dear,' she said approvingly, 'I was beginning to wonder if you were coming. Emma and her parents are waiting eagerly to meet you.'

He could feel his features tightening into a polite mask, and he made an effort to relax again. 'Hello, Rosie,' he teased softly. 'Don't waste any time, will you? Are you afraid I might do a bolt if I'm not hooked?'

Lady Rosemary's smile weakened. 'I do hope you're going to behave yourself, Will,' she countered severely, speaking in an undertone, so that the four other people dotted about the glass-covered verandah were unable to hear. 'Emma is not at all like Francesca Goddard, and I won't have you behaving as if she is.'

He sighed. 'What's that supposed to mean?' He paused. 'And by the way, Francesca still calls herself Francesca Quentin.'

'She would.' The old lady almost snorted the words. 'You know why, of course: she finds it useful. I'm surprised she hasn't attempted to retain the title, as well.'

She was scathing, and Will knew a moment's regret that this was so. He wondered if his parents, had they still been alive, would have regarded Francesca's behaviour with less censure. But they'd died in a freak boating accident when he was barely a teenager, and from then on his grandmother had been his guardian.

And from the beginning her attitude towards Francesca had always been vaguely hostile. He knew the old lady had never really considered Francesca good enough for him, and in any case she had had another, more socially and financially suitable candidate in mind. Unfortunately, he had been thinking with his heart and not his head in those days. He'd been crazy about Francesca; he'd wanted her; he'd wanted to marry her; and as far as he was concerned that had been that.

'Anyway, come along,' declared Lady Rosemary now, tucking her arm through his and turning to face her guests. 'Here he is, everyone. This is my grandson, William Quentin. Will, allow me to introduce Sir George and Lady Merritt, and their youngest daughter, Emma.'

Will had met people like the Merritts before. Sir George was a self-made man, a latter-day baronet, whose life peerage owed more to the worthy causes he supported than to any particular quality he possessed. He was several inches shorter than Will, with the rotund belly of a serious drinker, while his wife was thin to the point of emaciation, and obviously subscribed to the maxim that one couldn't be too thin or too rich.

Their daughter, he saw thankfully, was something else. Of all the young women his grandmother had produced for his inspection, Emma Merritt was by far the most attractive to date. Slim—without her mother's angularity—with straight silvery blonde hair that curved almost confidingly under her jawline, and wide blue eyes, she was quite startlingly good-looking, and he was impressed.

He caught his grandmother's eye on him at that moment, and he could almost see what the old lady was thinking. Lady Rosemary would take great pleasure in seeing her grandson married again, and introducing Emma as the new Countess of Lingard would restore her faith in her own beliefs. She wanted to see him settled; she wanted to know he had a family. Will guessed she was already considering how she could sponsor the children their union would produce.

Children?

Will's lips twisted with sudden cynicism, and Sir George Merritt regarded him with a certain amount of dismay. 'It's a great pleasure to meet you, my lord!' he exclaimed hastily, and Will struggled to regain his equanimity before disclaiming the older man's form of address.

'Quentin will do, Sir George,' he amended smoothly, earning a relieved smile for his trouble. 'Or Lingard, if you prefer. I seldom use my title among friends.'

Lady Merritt preened at the compliment, even as she protested his magnanimity. 'But you should,' she said coyly. 'Though we are flattered to be here.' And Will wondered with unwilling irony whether she was protecting his interests or her daughter's.

'My grandson has always been a law unto himself,' put in Lady Rosemary swiftly, perhaps aware of Will's response. 'When he was at college, he called himself Will Quentin, and no one knew his background.' She exchanged a speaking look with him again. 'I keep reminding him he has responsibilities he can't ignore.'

'To do with his rank, you mean,' Lady Merritt agreed, nodding. 'But, of course, we all have our particular crosses to bear. Take George, for instance: you can't imagine how often his services are called upon. There's always some charity dinner or benefit in the offing. He's become quite a popular after-dinner speaker.'

'I don't think that's what Lady Rosemary was talking about,' Emma interposed then, with a knowing smile. 'Perhaps—*he*—' she refrained from using either of the alternatives '—would rather people accepted him for himself,' she ventured, in an attractively breathy tone. 'I'd hate it if I thought my friends only cultivated me because I was your daughter, Daddy.'

Will had to smile at her audacity. In a couple of sentences, she had defused all their arguments, without causing any offence to anyone. She was obviously not as dumb as her appearance might have suggested, and he felt a little more optimistic about the evening ahead.

'Oh—well—' Sir George was the first to answer her. 'If you put it like that, my dear, I suppose I have to see your point.' He put an approving hand on her shoulder. 'Aren't I a lucky man—er—Lingard? A daughter with brains as well as beauty.'

'An unusual combination,' murmured Will drily, though after meeting Emma's artful gaze they weren't quite the sentiments he'd have chosen. Nevertheless, she was amusing, and far more interesting than some of the vapid débutante types he had had to deal with in the past.

The housemaid who had admitted him now reappeared carrying a tray of cocktails, but Will managed to avoid accepting one of his grandmother's concoctions. Instead, he sidled over to the table and helped himself to a measure of vintage Scotch, surveying his fellow guests over the rim of his glass.

He saw now that Archie Rossiter, one of his grandmother's elderly admirers, was dozing in a cane chair beside the winter cactus. Archie had been Lady Rosemary's doctor until he retired a couple of years ago, and he could always be relied upon to even the numbers, if required. He was a pleasant old man, if inclined to be a little forgetful these days. There was a whisky glass beside his chair, too, and Will guessed he'd been imbibing long before anyone else arrived. His lips twitched. Good old Archie! They might have had their differences at times, but he felt a certain amount of affection for the old man.

'Are we that boring?'

The voice came from close at hand, and he realised that while he had been studying Archie Rossiter Emma had left her parents talking to his grandmother, and come to join him.

'Boring?' he echoed, aware of her meaning but giving

himself time to think. 'Why should you think that, Miss Merritt? The evening's hardly begun.'

'Oh, I know that.' She regarded the cocktail she was holding for a moment, and then tilted her head to give him the full benefit of her wide-eyed gaze. 'And my name's Emma, not Miss Merritt. That sounds almost as dull as you probably think we are.'

Will arched one dark brow. 'You don't know what I think.'

'Don't I?' Clearly, she thought she did. 'You probably didn't want to join us for dinner, did you?'

'Why should you think that?'

It wasn't a denial, and he could tell from her expression that she knew it. 'Because Daddy was so insistent that he needed a few days in the country. You can never get him out of the office when we're at home.'

Will endeavoured to follow her conversation. 'And where is that?' he asked politely. 'Home, I mean? You're not from this area, I gather.'

'Hardly,' said Emma flatly. 'Or we wouldn't be staying at Mulberry Court. No, actually, we live in Cambridge. My father has business interests there.'

'Does he?'

Will forbore to ask what those business interests might be. He seemed to recall his grandmother mentioning something about microchip technology, and the uses to which it could be put in mobile phones and fax machines. According to Lady Rosemary—and this was the important thing so far as she was concerned—Sir George was incredibly wealthy, and eager to acquire for his youngest daughter the kind of pedigree money couldn't buy.

'Lady Rosemary told us you studied at Cambridge,' Emma continued, and he wondered exactly how much she knew of the unholy alliance to which her father aspired. 'Unfortunately, I wasn't clever enough to go to university,' she added. 'So Daddy sent me to a finishing school in Switzerland instead.'

Will's mouth flattened. 'I can't believe you couldn't have found a place at university if you'd really wanted to,' he remarked drily, and was rewarded by a mischievous glance out of the corner of her eye.

'Well, who wants to spend hours studying stuffy old books when one could be out riding or swimming or watching polo?' she declared smugly. 'It was so much more fun in Lausanne. You wouldn't believe the things we got up to.'

Will thought he probably could, but he didn't comment, and presently she began to talk about the history of Mulberry Court and how much she enjoyed exploring old buildings. After what she'd said about the stuffiness of books and study, Will doubted she had any real interest in the subject—not in an objective way, at least. But he knew what was expected of him, and politely suggested she might like to visit the Abbey while she was here, and he knew from the enthusiasm of her acceptance that he was right.

By the time Mrs Baxter, his grandmother's housekeeper, came to announce that supper was ready, he felt he knew virtually all there was to know about Emma's life up to that point. He knew the schools she'd attended, the subjects she'd enjoyed most, and her tentative plans for the future. The fact that she was keen to fall in love and get married, and subsequently have a large family, had been relayed to him in that attractively breathy tone, and he doubted few men would remain immune to such appealing candour.

Somewhat to his relief, he found Archie Rossiter on his left at supper. The heavy table, which had once occupied a central position in the dining hall, was now used as a sideboard, and the table they ate from was of a much more manageable size. Acting on his grandmother's instructions, he was sure, Mrs Baxter had placed Will beside Emma Merritt, thus enabling Lady Rosemary to have Sir George and his daughter on either hand.

It was obvious the old lady intended to keep a sharp eye on the young woman she was hoping might become her grandson's wife, but it suited Will's purposes very well. He could parry any awkward questions by talking to the old man, and with Lady Merritt sitting opposite this was no small advantage.

And yet he wasn't totally opposed to being scrutinised in his turn, and whenever his grandmother caught his eye he turned a tolerant smile in her direction. He had invited Emma to Lingard; he would see how things developed from there. He was making no impetuous promises he couldn't keep.

He ate sparingly, finding the cook's reliance on garlic and rich Mediterranean sauces hard to stomach. But Luisa was Italian, and didn't take kindly to being criticised, and his grandmother was afraid to offend her in case she left. It wasn't easy keeping staff in Yorkshire, when the lure of London and higher wages was so attractive. But Luisa had family in the neighbourhood, and the fact that Lady Rosemary spent the early part of the year in London anyway enabled her to enjoy the best of both worlds.

Besides, as his grandmother was known to argue, what was wrong with pasta and tomatoes? They were both good, wholesome ingredients, and far better for you than stodgy pies and puddings. He looked down at his plate, his lips tightening, as he remembered sharing a joke with Francesca about Luisa's temperamental nature. His ex-wife had expressed the view that if Luisa produced pasta pies and puddings Lady Rosemary wouldn't say a word against them.

'I understand you spent some time on our home territory,' Lady Merritt interrupted him now, and for a moment Will didn't know what she meant. 'At Cambridge,' she added pointedly. 'Wasn't that where you took your degree?'

Will drew a breath. 'Oh—Cambridge,' he said politely. 'Yes. That's right. But it's some years ago now. I've almost forgotten my college days.'

'Not that long ago,' inserted Lady Rosemary, proving she was not above eavesdropping herself if she felt it was needed. 'You're only thirty-four, Will. You talk as if it was the dim and distant past.' She paused, and then added with rather more asperity, 'I can imagine there are aspects of that time that are rather—disagreeable to you. But don't dismiss your education.' She glanced around to include the whole table in her next words. 'It's so important, don't you think?'

'Well—'

Lady Merritt was less positive on this subject, and Emma took the opportunity to explain why. 'I'm afraid I've been quite a disappointment in that department, Lady Rosemary. I have to admit, I couldn't wait to leave school.'

'But she had extremely good marks while she was there—' began her mother, only to be overridden again in her turn.

'I was talking about my grandson,' said Lady Rosemary, managing to modify her comments without giving offence. She bestowed a brilliant smile on Emma, and then continued, 'I wouldn't want another bluestocking for a granddaughter-in-law, my dear. Believe me, one was quite enough.'

She had gone too far. Will knew she had sensed her mistake long before she encountered her grandson's cool grey stare. Which was why she hurried on to another topic, asking Sir George what he thought of the local golf club where he had played a round that afternoon.

'Was your wife very clever?' enquired Emma artlessly, and, although her questions had amused him before, now he felt a sense of impatience.

'Not particularly,' he answered shortly, taking refuge in his glass of wine. Though the truth was that Francesca had been rather clever—too clever for her own good, he thought bitterly, refilling his glass.

'I hear your man's had some success with his fuchsias this year,' Archie Rossiter remarked amiably, jolting Will out of his darkening mood, and he turned gratefully towards the old man.

'I'm pleased to hear he's had some success with something,' he said forcefully. 'He lost a pair of electric shears this afternoon. He's always leaving his tools lying about, and then expressing surprise when they disappear.'

Archie chuckled. 'He's getting old, Will. We all are. Your grandmother included, only she'd never admit it.'

'Is that her excuse?' queried Will wryly, and Archie pulled a sympathetic face.

'Probably. Though, as I said, she'd be the last to say so.'

'To say what?' demanded Lady Rosemary, overhearing them, but then subsided again when she met her grandson's eyes. 'Oh, well,' she muttered, pressing her palms together and surveying her other guests with determined brightness. 'Shall we adjourn to the drawing room for coffee?'

Will made his escape soon after nine-thirty.

His taste for conspiracy had palled somewhat, and although he had agreed to pick Emma and her parents up the following morning and bring them back to the Abbey for lunch he was more than ready to relinquish their company tonight.

It was still light as he drove back to the Abbey, and the scents of wild blossom and newly mown hay were a balm to his restless spirit. He was tempted to call at the pub in Lingard village and enjoy a pint of beer with the landlord, but the knowledge that he would have to drive back to the Abbey afterwards deterred him. He'd already drunk more than enough this evening, and with the prospect of playing host tomorrow ahead of him he decided he would be advised to be temperate.

The outline of the Abbey was visible long before he reached the park gates. Its grey stone walls were clearly silhouetted against the amber sky, and he knew a momentary sense of pride that his ancestors had lived here for more than two hundred years. There had actually been a monastery on the site for much longer than that, but that had been destroyed during the dissolution that had taken place in the sixteenth century. The present building owed its origins to the early part of the seventeenth century, with successive occupants making additions and alterations to its ivy-hung façde. Although it was by no means a luxurious residence, certain comforts such as central heating had made the old place infinitely more habitable. It would be a shame, he thought ruefully, if it was allowed to deteriorate even more. He owed it to himself, and to Lingard, to do everything in his power to prevent that from happening.

He frowned when he saw the small sports car parked on the gravelled sweep in front of the house. He wasn't expecting any visitors, and none of the servants owned such a vehicle. It was possible that it was some relative of theirs who was visiting, but he couldn't imagine Watkins allowing anyone to park in front of the building.

He certainly wasn't in the mood to be sociable with anyone, and, jamming on the brakes, he brought the Range Rover to a halt beside the offending car. Whoever it was had better have a bloody good excuse, he thought aggressively, vaulting out of his seat. Slamming the door, he strode towards the house. The forecourt wasn't a car park, after all.

The heavy door opened to his hand, proving that Watkins had not yet got around to locking up. Inside, the stone floor of the vestibule threw up a chill after the warmth of the air outside, but he scarcely noticed the difference as he pressed on into the vaulted hall.

Here, worn Persian rugs helped to mitigate the chill that emanated from the thick walls. The walls themselves were hung with fading tapestries, which offered little in the way of warmth or comfort, but they were familiar, and Will was loath to part with them. He had already sold everything of any real value in his efforts to keep the old place going, and the threadbare hangings were an integral part of his heritage.

He had halted in the doorway to the small family parlour, and was scowling at the fact that in his absence someone had taken the liberty of lighting a fire in the grate, when he heard Watkins' wheezing breath behind him.

'Oh, my lord!' he exclaimed, and it was obvious from his expression that he knew what to expect. 'You're back!'

'It would appear so,' remarked Will, with forced cordiality. 'Do you mind telling me what the hell is going on?'

Watkins patted his chest with his gnarled fist, as if by doing so he could relieve the congestion that had gathered there, and offered his employer an appealing look. 'You've—er—you've got a visitor, my lord,' he said hoarsely. 'She—she arrived just after you'd left.'

'She?'

For the life of him, Will couldn't think of any female who might turn up on his doorstep unannounced, but before Watkins could marshal his explanations a disturbingly familiar voice interrupted them. 'Hello, Will,' he heard with unbelieving ears. 'I hoped you wouldn't mind if I made myself at home.'

CHAPTER TWO

FRANCESCA!

Will turned with stunned eyes to see his ex-wife crossing the hall towards him. Rocking back on his heels, he stared at her as if he'd never seen her before, and certainly she looked much different from the woman he remembered.

Gone were the jeans and casual clothes she'd regularly worn, and in their place was an elegant navy business suit and high-heeled pumps. Her long, slender legs—one of the first things that had attracted him to her, he remembered unwillingly—were encased in gossamer-thin navy tights, and her hair, which she'd always worn loose, was confined in a tight knot at the back of her head. Her features, thinner than he remembered, surely, were thrown into sharp relief by the severity of her hairstyle, but if the intention had been to maximise the austerity of her appearance she had not succeeded. On the contrary, she looked quite wildly beautiful, a sensuous, sensual woman wrapped up in a sombre shell.

'That—that's what I was trying to tell you, my lord,' Watkins mumbled, watching his employer's reaction with anxious eyes. 'Miss—Mrs—um—your wife arrived earlier this evening. I hope you don't mind: I had Mrs Harvey prepare the guest suite in the west wing.'

Will was tempted to remind the old man that Francesca wasn't his wife any more, but it was obvious from his fumbling form of address that he hadn't forgotten. 'It's Mrs Quentin,' he said. And then, arching a brow at Francesca he asked, 'That is still how you like to be addressed?'

19

'It will do,' she agreed, with a tightening of her lips. 'How are you, Will? I must say, you look well.'

'Thank you.' Will didn't return the compliment, even if the awareness of her sophisticated appearance hung between them with an almost tangible air. 'Do you want to tell me what you're doing here, Francesca? I don't remember issuing an invitation, and I'm afraid it's not particularly convenient right now.'

The muscles in her cheeks contracted, almost as if he had hit her, and Will knew an unwarranted sense of guilt at the sight. Dammit, he thought, she ought not to have come here. He didn't owe her anything. If she was short of money, she'd certainly come to the wrong place.

'If you'll excuse me, my lord.' Watkins was of the old school, where it was never polite to be rude to a lady. Particularly not a lady who had once lived at Lingard Abbey, who had shared every aspect of his employer's life, his ambitions, his bed...

'Mrs—er—Mrs Harvey has prepared some sandwiches, my lord,' he added swiftly, gesturing into the room behind Will. 'There's some tea—um—Mrs Quentin preferred it to coffee. Shall I fetch another cup?'

'That won't be necessary,' said Will shortly, aware that he was behaving unnecessarily boorishly, but unable to do anything about it. For God's sake, he thought, he'd got Emma and her parents coming for lunch tomorrow. Imagine having to tell them that he was playing host to his ex-wife.

'Then if that's all, my lord...'

'Of course, of course.' Will strove for normality and, avoiding looking at Francesca, he gave Watkins a constrained smile. 'You get along to bed,' he dismissed the old man pleasantly. 'Oh—and perhaps you'd inform Mrs Harvey there'll be three guests for lunch tomorrow.'

Watkins' eyes darted to Francesca in some perplexity. '*Three* guests, my lord?'

'Excluding Mrs Quentin,' said Will flatly. 'Goodnight, Watkins. I'll make sure the doors are locked.'

Watkins nodded, offered Francesca a somewhat awkward farewell, and ambled off towards the leather-studded door that gave access to the kitchen and servants' quarters. He walked slowly and Will had to stifle his impatience, but once the heavy door had swung to behind him he allowed Francesca the full weight of his frustration. 'What the hell do you think you're doing?' he snapped. 'The Abbey is not a private hotel. You can't just turn up here when it suits you. You walked out, Francesca. Lingard is no longer your home.'

'I know that.' Francesca crossed her arms at her waist and wrapped them about herself, almost as if she was cold. She looked beyond him, into the lamplit room, where the fire was glowing so invitingly. 'Can't we sit down, at least?'

Will glanced over his shoulder. As Watkins had said, Mrs Harvey had prepared a tray of tea and sandwiches, and it was presently waiting on the carved chest beside the sofa. It had apparently been placed there while Francesca was—where? Being shown to her room? Settling in? His jaw hardened. It irritated him that she should have come here. She had no rights where he, or this house, was concerned.

But something, some latent spark of humanity, perhaps, prevented him from asking her to leave at once. One night, he thought, but in the morning she was out of here. He had no desire to renew their acquaintance, whatever she might think.

Nevertheless, he stepped aside to allow her to enter the parlour, and she brushed past him with evident relief. If he hadn't known better, he'd have said she was on the edge of hysteria. But Francesca didn't have nerves; she was always in control of her emotions.

He hesitated before joining her. It was obvious he was going to have to speak to her at some time, but he objected to being forced to accommodate her tonight. Yet if he left it until the morning who knew how soon he would get rid of her? And with the Merritts expecting him at eleven he didn't have a lot of time to spare.

So, despite his unwillingness, he pushed his hands into the pockets of his jacket and followed her into the room. But he deliberately left the door open. He had nothing to hide, and if she did it was just hard luck.

Francesca had seated herself on the sofa, at the end nearest the fire, and Will was surprised. Although it was a warm night outside, the parlour was cool, but as she was wearing a suit he wouldn't have expected her to be cold. Yet it seemed as if she was. Every line of her hunched form pointed to it. And, although she helped herself to a cup of tea, she made no attempt to touch the sandwiches.

The parlour was not a large room by the Abbey's standards, and the heat from the grate caused Will to loosen the collar of his shirt and pull the knot of his tie an inch or two away. He would have taken off his jacket, but he didn't want her to get the impression that he was comfortable with the situation, so he remained where he was, behind the sofa opposite, with the width of the hearth between them.

'Aren't you going to sit down?' she asked, glancing up at him, her elbows resting on her silk-clad knees, the teacup cradled between her palms. Her drawn features mirrored the anxiety that was evident in her eyes, and although he chided himself for feeling any sympathy for her he came around the sofa and straddled its hide-covered arm.

'Okay,' he said coolly. 'I'm sitting down. So, what is this all about? I should warn you, Francesca, I'm not in the mood to play games. If you've got something to say, then for God's sake get on with it.'

Her nostrils flared at his insensitivity, and once again Will felt a reluctant sense of compassion. It seemed that, whatever had brought her back to the Abbey she was either too ashamed—or too apprehensive of his reaction—to tell him, and she was looking for his support, not his sarcasm.

'I drove up from London this evening,' she ventured, and twin creases bracketed his mouth.

'Yes, I gathered that,' he said, wondering what this was leading to. 'I assume that is your car parked on the forecourt.'

'Well, it's a friend's car, actually,' she offered, and his mouth flattened as he wondered which particular friend that was. Male, he assumed; Francesca had always had plenty of men friends. Though there were a couple of girls she had shared rooms with at college whom she'd used to keep in touch with. 'I thought it was less likely to be noticed,' she added. 'He—er—he knows my registration, you see.'

Will's brows drew together. 'Who are we talking about now?' he asked tersely. 'This—friend?'

'What friend? Oh—you mean the car!' Francesca sipped her tea. 'No, that belongs to Clare—one of the women I work with.'

Will tried not to get impatient. 'What's wrong with your own car? Has it broken down?' His eyes narrowed. 'If that's what this is about—'

'As if!' Francesca stared at him disgustedly. 'Do you honestly think I'd have come to you if all I wanted to do was change my car?'

'I don't know, do I?' Will's eyes hardened. 'Perhaps the problem is I can't imagine anything that I might be willing to do for you,' he retorted sharply. 'And if some man is giving you grief, think again!'

The china teacup clattered into its saucer, and spots of brown liquid dotted the white cloth. For a moment, he thought she must have burned her mouth, but then he realised she was crying. Huge, shuddering sobs were shaking her thin shoulders, and she'd wrapped her arms about her knees and was rocking back and forth, like a child in pain.

Will stared at her, aghast. In all the years he had

known her, he had never known Francesca to cry—not like this, at least. Even when they'd split up, she had maintained a mask of indifference when she was with him, and if her eyelids had sometimes looked puffy he'd put it down to lack of sleep.

But this—this was different. Whatever was wrong with her it was something she obviously couldn't handle herself. The thought that she might have discovered she had some terminal disease caused a shaft of pain inside him.

But something had to be done now. He had to say something, do something, to bring her out of this paroxysm of grief. She'd regret giving in and letting him see her this way, once she was over it, he thought cynically. But he didn't think it was an act. Playing for sympathy wasn't Francesca's style.

Or it hadn't been. He scowled. Dammit, it was more than five years since he'd seen her, and anything could have happened to her in that time. But he didn't think she could have changed her personality. She'd lost weight, sure, but she didn't strike him as having lost her self-respect.

'Fran,' he said persuasively, the name he had had for her sliding automatically off his tongue. 'Hey,' he added, his spread fingers curling impotently over his thighs, 'it can't be that serious. Come on. Lighten up. I didn't mean what I said.'

'Didn't you?'

Her head had been buried in her hands, but now her fingers parted to reveal drowned amber eyes. She still shook, but the aching sobs had eased somewhat, and he wondered if he was in danger of being treated as a fool all over again.

'Perhaps not,' he muttered, in two minds as to how to deal with this, and she fumbled in the purse at her feet for a tissue to dry her face. 'Fran—Francesca—what is going on? Are you going to tell me?' He balled one fist inside the other. 'I gather the problem is some man.'

She nodded then, scrubbing at her eyes with the tissue as Will felt a rekindling of his anger. Dammit, he thought, what did she think he was? Some kind of agony husband? *Ex*-husband, he amended harshly. Any problems she had, she should deal with herself.

'It's not what you think,' she said at last, when she had herself in control again, and Will arched a sceptical brow.

'No?' he queried flatly. And then he said, 'You've admitted it's a man, haven't you? How many distinctions are there?'

'Quite a lot, actually,' she answered quickly, using the tissue to blow her nose. 'I didn't say it was a man I've been involved with.' She shivered. 'As a matter of fact, we've never even met.'

'What?' Will hooked his leg over the arm and slid down onto the sofa proper. 'What are you saying? That some man is pestering you?' He felt a disproportionate sense of anger. 'For pity's sake, Fran, why haven't you reported him to the police?'

'I have.' She drew a trembling breath. 'There's nothing they can do.'

'Don't be ridiculous! Of course there's something they can do. They can arrest the man. If he's giving you a hard time, that's all the proof they need.'

'No, it's not.' Francesca's shoulders drooped. 'Being—pestered by someone doesn't constitute a felony. In any case, they don't know who he is.'

'You haven't told them?'

'I don't know who it is,' she retorted huskily. 'He— I—he's too clever to let them catch him in the act.'

Will stared at her. 'In the act of what?' His stomach tightened. 'Has he touched you?'

'Not yet,' answered Francesca in an uneven tone. 'I've told you, we've never met. But—I think he's tried to break into my flat.' Her abhorrence was apparent. 'That's when I knew I had to get away.'

Will sank back against the squashy upholstery, disbelief warring with a growing sense of outrage. It couldn't be true, he told himself. Francesca was lying; she had to be. It was inconceivable that her life was in any kind of danger.

Swallowing the bile that had gathered at the back of his throat, he regarded her steadily. 'Perhaps you ought to tell me how long this has been going on,' he suggested, propping one booted foot beside the tray, and she nodded.

'Yes.' She moistened her lips. 'Well—about six months, I suppose, altogether. To begin with, I didn't know what was going on.'

Will breathed deeply. 'Six months!' he said. 'So long?'

'Well, according to the police, a stalker can take years before he approaches his victim. To begin with, he gets his kicks from watching them without them knowing what's going on.'

Will blew back the hair from his forehead. Despite himself, he was responding to the frankness of her tone. If she was lying, she was making a bloody good job of it. And if she wasn't— His lips tightened. Frustration didn't even begin to cover how he felt.

'Go on,' he said, not trusting himself to make any constructive comment, and, resting her arms along her thighs, she shredded the tissue she was holding as she continued.

'At first—at first I thought I was imagining it. As you probably know, I'm still working for Teniko, and just recently—within the last year, that is—my hours have been changed. Sometimes, I start later in the morning, but I don't get home until later in the evening.'

'Why?'

She flushed. 'Because—because I've been promoted. And Teniko have moved their head office to California, which means we often have satellite conferences in the evening.'

'In the evening?' Will knew it wasn't important, and

he was perfectly aware why the meetings would be so late. But he needed a little time to come to terms with this, and talking about normal things, like her working hours, enabled him to get some perspective.

'It's morning in San Francisco,' Francesca explained, answering him anyway. 'We're presently involved in developing some new computer software, and as the virtual reality market is a very competitive field our meetings are always confidential.'

'I don't want to hear about your job,' said Will shortly, and he was annoyed to hear the irritation in his voice. He didn't want her to think he cared a damn what she was doing with her life, but at the same time he didn't want her to think he was bitter either. He wiped his expression clean of any emotion before asking evenly, 'Are you saying you're alone when you leave the building?'

Francesca nodded. 'Sometimes. At least, there are very few other commuters about. The rush hour's over, you see. Most people have already left their offices. And—and it's much easier to follow someone if they're not tied up in a crowd.'

'Easier for you to see them, too,' Will commented, not at all convinced by that argument.

'Only if they want to be seen,' said Francesca, moistening her lips. 'I don't always see him, but I know that he's there.'

'I see.' Will watched the way she pulled out another tissue and proceeded to shred it, also. 'So—this man, whoever he is, follows you.' He made an impatient sound. 'You're saying the police can't do anything about that?'

Francesca sniffed. 'I'm not sure they even believe me.'

'Why not?'

'Because they've never seen him.' She swallowed. 'He's very clever, Will. Sometimes—sometimes I used to think I was going mad.'

Will breathed deeply. He wanted to dismiss what she was saying. He wanted to tell her he didn't believe her either, and leave her to deal with her own life. But he couldn't. Truth to tell, the strongest urge he had was to vault across the carved chest, with its tray of tea and sandwiches, and go and comfort her. To pull her into his arms and tell her not to worry; he would handle it.

Instead, he scooped up a couple of the smoked salmon sandwiches Mrs Harvey had prepared for Francesca's supper, and ate them. He was suddenly fiendishly hungry. Probably because he'd eaten so little at Mulberry Court. He refused to countenance any other explanation for his hunger, despite the connotations. He was not eating to compensate for any other need.

'It's true,' she said, evidently deciding that this tackling of the food signalled a certain scepticism on his part. 'I always know when he's following me. It's a funny feeling—a kind of sixth sense a woman has. Only—' she scrubbed at her cheeks again '—there's nothing remotely funny about it.'

'And that's all he does? Follow you?'

'He did.'

'Has anyone else seen him?'

'Only my landlady.' She hesitated. 'She was in the flat one evening, when I saw him standing outside the building. He was wearing one of those black hoods at the time. I couldn't see his face.'

'So how did you know it was him?'

'Because I recognised the way he was dressed.' She gazed at him frantically. 'He always wears a hooded jacket. One of those brushed cotton jackets, I think it is, that people wear for jogging.'

'Perhaps he is a jogger?'

The look she gave him was bleak. 'He follows me, Will. Don't you understand? He enjoys frightening me. I've taken books out of the library to try and understand what he gets out of it. It's the element of uncertainty—of fear—that gives him the most pleasure.'

Will hesitated. 'The night you saw him—outside your apartment, you said—didn't you call the police then?'

'What would have been the use? There's no law that says a man can't stand in the street. I've even started using my car for work, instead of getting the bus. But he always knows where to find me.'

Will knew an almost uncontrollable sense of fury, a raw anger that simmered in his gut. He didn't want to be, but he could feel himself being drawn into this. He might not want her as his wife any longer, but he was damned if he was going to let her be terrified to death by some pervert.

'Eventually—eventually, I started getting phone calls,' she went on, her voice growing thinner. 'You know the sort of thing—starting off with heavy breathing and progressing from there. I bought an answering machine, in the hope that that would stop him, but it didn't. When I came home some evenings, there were maybe half a dozen of his messages waiting on the tape.'

Will swore. 'The police must have taken notice of you then.'

'Oh, yes. They did. They advised me to change my number.' Her lips quivered. 'Then it started all over again.'

Will blinked. 'He got your new number? How? God, it must be someone you know!'

'No.' She trembled. 'I think he must have got into the apartment. There's no other way we could think of to explain how that had happened.'

Will stiffened. 'We?'

'Yes, we.' Francesca tried to compose herself. 'Tom Radley. He's a friend. He works at Teniko, too.'

Will nodded, aware that his reaction to the fact that she had a man friend wasn't exactly dispassionate. Yet why shouldn't she have an admirer? he asked himself. He hadn't exactly lived the life of a monk since she'd left.

'We are just friends,' Francesca asserted now, and Will wondered if his expression had given him away.

'Hey, that's your affair,' he said lightly, managing to sound almost indifferent. 'I'm glad you've got some support. That helps a lot.'

'No, it doesn't.' She gazed at him with tear-wet eyes, and he despised himself for thinking that she still looked good in spite of her distress. 'Tom's offered to move in, but I don't want him to. We don't have that kind of a relationship and I don't want him to get the wrong idea.'

Will looked down at his spread hands, aware that this was getting harder by the minute. For God's sake, he thought, why had she come to him? If she imagined he might offer to move in with her, she was wrong.

'The calls,' he said quickly, desperate to distract himself from sensual images of what it had been like when he and Francesca had lived together. 'Couldn't they be traced?'

'Oh, sure.' Francesca moved her hand. 'They were made from call boxes all over the city. There was never any pattern to them. He's much too clever to get caught out like that.'

'And the voice isn't familiar?'

She shuddered. 'No.'

'And when you decided he'd been in your apartment...' He paused. 'I assume you changed all the locks?'

'Yes.'

There was an exhausted note to her voice now, and, looking at her, he realised how tired she must be. If she'd done a day's work and then driven up here, she must be absolutely worn out. He should let her get some sleep before continuing this inquisition. And yet...

'You say you didn't want to stay in the apartment,' he persisted. 'Yet you obviously stayed there after you thought he'd broken in.' He bit his lip. 'What happened tonight that so upset you? I know I sound as if I'm playing devil's advocate, but I just want to know why you felt you had to get away.'

Francesca expelled a trembling breath. 'When I got home from work tonight, I found the bathroom window had been broken.' She fought for control. 'That was bad enough, but then—then the phone rang, just as I was examining the damage. It was him. The stalker.' She shuddered. 'He said—he said he was watching me. I—I asked him if he'd broken my window and he said that I shouldn't bother to get it mended because he'd be back.'

CHAPTER THREE

FRANCESCA had never slept in one of the Abbey's guest suites.

Even before she and Will were married, when she had stayed for several weeks at Lingard, she'd always slept with him—in his suite, in his bed. Of course, when their relationship had become intolerable, Will had moved into one of the other suites himself. But she had always occupied the principal apartments, and it was odd to find herself in unfamiliar surroundings now.

Not that they were unwelcome surroundings, she acknowledged wearily, sinking down onto the side of the canopied bed. At least here she didn't constantly feel the urge to look over her shoulder, and she could go to sleep without being afraid of either phone calls or unwanted intruders.

She shivered.

It had been crazy to come here, though. In all honesty, she still didn't know why she'd come to Will. Except that when she'd found the window broken, and then taken that awful call, she'd panicked. It was as if she'd reached a kind of breaking point herself, as if the knowledge that *he* could even see her in her own flat was the last straw. Until then, she'd regarded her apartment as a sanctuary. Despite the fear that he might have broken in, she'd had no proof. But suddenly she'd lost any sense of security. She doubted she'd ever feel the same about the place again.

When she'd first left Will, she'd been forced to live in a bed-sitter, and after the clean air and space she had found at the Abbey, the room, in a hostel off Edgware Road, had seemed dark and poky. If he'd come after her then, if he'd shown even the slightest hint that he still cared for her, she'd have gone back to him, willingly. She'd have swallowed her pride and returned to Yorkshire without a second's hesitation.

But, of course, he hadn't. Will had his pride, too. Her lips twisted. God, he'd been full of it. Still was, if she was honest enough to admit it. He might have sympathised with her dilemma tonight, but he didn't really want her here.

Perhaps she should have accepted Clare's invitation to stay with her. She lived just a few streets away from Francesca's home in Harmsworth Gardens, and at least that would have enabled her to go to work tomorrow. As it was, she would have to think of a convincing excuse for her boss at Teniko. He hadn't been particularly sympathetic when she'd told him of her problems before.

Still, tomorrow was Friday, and with a bit of luck she'd be feeling more herself by Monday morning. She knew she hadn't been thinking too clearly when she'd begged Clare for the loan of her Mazda just hours ago. All she'd felt was an overpowering need to get away from London, and she'd come to Will because he was someone she could trust.

And that was an irony, too, she mused bitterly, remembering how little he'd trusted her when she'd walked out. Why had she come to him, when he'd always been so willing to think the worst of her? Why had she sought his protection before that of anyone else?

Maybe if she'd had close family of her own it would have been different, she reflected. But, like Will, she'd lost both her parents before she was old enough to leave school. She'd not been as young as Will when he'd lost his parents, but she'd had no fairy grandmother to come to her rescue. Just her mother's elderly aunt, who'd considered caring for her orphaned niece a duty, but not a pleasure.

Francesca drew a heavy breath and pushed herself up from the mattress. The temptation was just to sit there and feel sorry for herself, but she ought to try and get some sleep. Will had said to relax, that they would talk again in the morning. But in spite of being bone-tired her mind wouldn't let her rest.

She caught sight of her reflection in the mirror which topped a skirted dressing table and, moving nearer, she examined her features with a critical stare. Her eyes were puffy, and she smoothed the veined skin below them with unsteady fingers. She looked older than Will this evening, she thought disconsolately. He'd always used to say his two years' seniority could have been ten.

The bag Watkins had brought up earlier was resting on a padded ottoman, and, unzipping the top, she pulled out her toilet bag and the nightshirt she wore to sleep in. Apart from these items, jeans, underwear and a couple of shirts comprised her whole wardrobe. There was little point in hanging them up. They wouldn't take up an eighth of the space in the enormous clothes closet.

The adjoining bathroom was equally huge. Francesca washed and cleaned her teeth at the large porcelain handbasin, promising herself that she would use the clawfooted bath in the morning, when she didn't feel so deathly weak. Her face looked pale and drawn, and she impatiently pulled the pins out of her hair so that it fell in crinkled disorder about her shoulders. At least it softened her profile, she thought, contenting herself with just threading her fingers through its thickness tonight.

She was sliding between the crisp linen sheets of the brass bed when there was a knock at her door. In spite of herself, she automatically started, her stomach churning and her heart thumping heavily in her chest. But then the realisation of where she was, and the expectation of who it might be, reassured her. It was probably Mrs Harvey, to see if she had everything she needed.

'C-come in,' she called, annoyed to hear the tremor in her voice even so, but she forgot her irritation when Will stepped into the room.

'I thought you might like a drink,' he said flatly, and

her eyes darted to the mug in his hand. 'I'm sorry if I frightened you. It's just hot milk. It might help you to sleep.'

'Thanks.' Francesca shuffled into a comfortable position against the pillows, making sure the sheet was securely covering her chest. She took the mug. 'This is very kind of you. I can't remember the last time I had hot milk.'

Will arched a speculative brow. 'Don't you like it?'

'I didn't say that.' She took a sip of the steaming beverage and then licked a smear of whiteness from her lip. 'I just meant it's a long time since—since I've been offered any.' She'd nearly said since anyone had looked after her. She looked up at him, somewhat awkwardly. 'I'm sorry I'm being such a nuisance. I—didn't know where else to go.'

'It's no problem,' he assured her evenly, and started back towards the door. 'I'll see you in the morning. Just tell Mrs Harvey if you'd like your breakfast in bed.'

'I shan't—' she began, but the door had already closed behind his lean form, and she was left to take what comfort she could from the milk. But at least it showed he had some compassion for her, she thought wryly. In his position, would she have been so understanding with her ex?

If it was Will, probably, she decided ruefully, taking another mouthful of the hot milk. In spite of everything that had happened, she still found him disturbingly attractive. Physically, at least, she amended swiftly. Which wasn't the same as how she'd felt before.

All the same...

She sniffed and drank some more, gasping as the unwary gulp of liquid burnt the back of her throat. Dammit, she thought, her eyes watering, he was just a man, wasn't he? And after her experiences of the past few months she ought to have more sense.

She slept at once. As soon as her head touched the pillow, she was dead to the world, and it wasn't until she saw sunlight pushing its way between the cracks in the curtains that she pondered the possibility that Will had put something more than just hot milk in her mug the night before.

Whatever, she awakened feeling relaxed, and vastly more optimistic. She almost managed to convince herself that nothing could be quite as bad as she'd imagined, although once again, when someone tapped for admittance, her nerves tightened uncontrollably, and it was an effort to speak.

This time it was Mrs Harvey, with a tray of morning tea, and she regarded her erstwhile mistress with surprising compassion. Francesca would have expected the housekeeper to resent her being here; she had no doubt Will's grandmother would. Lady Rosemary had never wanted Will to marry her, and finding her here now she would be bound to think the worst.

But Mrs Harvey took the sight of her employer's ex-wife in her stride. Even though Francesca was fresh out of the shower—she had eschewed the delights of the bath in favour of a speedier alternative—with one of the fluffy white towels tucked hurriedly beneath her arms, she showed no bias. 'His lordship asked me to enquire if you'd care to take breakfast in the morning room,' she announced, setting the tray on one of the square bedside cabinets before straightening to face her. 'Might I say, you look much more yourself this morning, madam. We were all quite concerned about you last night.'

Francesca wondered what Will had told them. She'd forgotten how much a part of the family the servants at the Abbey considered themselves, and although Mrs Harvey was in her late fifties she was still one of the younger members of the staff. The trouble was, most of Will's employees had been at the Abbey since before he was born, and it was difficult maintaining any kind of detachment with people who had once dandled you on their knee.

'Oh—I'm fine,' she assured Mrs Harvey now. 'And I

would prefer to come down for breakfast. But just toast and coffee for me, if you don't mind,' she added, remembering the housekeeper's penchant for eggs and bacon. 'And thank you for the tea.'

'Are you sure that's all you want? Just toast and coffee? His lordship has fruit juice and cereal as well.'

'I'm sure,' said Francesca firmly. 'Will fifteen minutes be all right?' She touched her damp hair. 'Oh, and do you have a drier?'

It turned out that there was a hair-drier in the dressing-table drawer, and after Mrs Harvey had left Francesca plugged it in. She was aware that the housekeeper would have liked to stay and chat, but thankfully her duties prevented her from wasting any more time.

Francesca drank a cup of tea between bouts of drying her hair. It was getting too long, she reflected wryly, aware that it was probably more trouble than it was worth. She'd always had thick curly hair, and when she was a student she used to wear it loose. But these days she almost always secured it in a knot. Her employers at Teniko did not like untidy hair.

Deciding she was not at work today, and that she could afford to be a little more adventurous, she eventually twisted it into a chunky plait. At least it made her look a little younger, she thought, though she didn't know why that should be an advantage. It wasn't as if she wanted to impress Will. He was far too cynical for that.

She dressed in her jeans and a bronze silk shirt that was almost exactly the same colour as her hair. Thankfully, she had stuffed a pair of Doc Martens at the bottom of the bag, so she put them on without any socks. At least they looked better than her high-heeled pumps.

She hesitated about making her bed, and then decided against it. She remembered there were definite lines of demarcation at the Abbey, and guests did not appropriate other people's jobs. It was something she had found hard to get used to when she'd first come to live at Lingard, but by the time she left she had become as accustomed to the privilege as Will himself.

Leaving her room, she walked along the corridor to the galleried landing, and then descended the shallow carpeted staircase to the vestibule below. The row of portraits of Will's ancestors that lined the walls seemed to regard her disapprovingly. They probably took their cue from Lady Rosemary, thought Francesca wryly. There was a definite look of disdain in their blank stares. She shivered. She was getting paranoiac. She was imagining people were watching her wherever she went.

The house felt decidedly chilly at this hour of the morning, before the warmth of the day had had time to penetrate its thick walls. She half wished she had brought a sweater, but she hadn't considered such practicalities when she'd packed her bag. She consoled herself with the thought that the morning room faced south-east, and was probably much warmer than the hall.

Will was still seated at the square breakfast table when she entered the sunlit apartment. She had half expected him to be gone; she had taken much longer than the fifteen minutes she had promised Mrs Harvey. But, although he had apparently had his breakfast, he was presently occupied with opening the morning's post. A copy of the morning newspaper, too, was crumpled beside his plate.

Telling herself she had no reason to be nervous of him, Francesca nevertheless hesitated in the open doorway. 'Um—good morning,' she ventured, instantly attracting his attention. 'I'm sorry I've taken so long.'

'No problem.' Stuffing the invoice he had been holding back into its envelope, Will got immediately to his feet. 'Sit down,' he said. 'Mrs Harvey's getting you some toast. But the coffee's still hot if you'd like some.'

'Thanks.' A place had been laid for her at right angles to his, and Francesca subsided awkwardly into her seat. In the light of day, her fears of the night before seemed much exaggerated, and she made a determined effort to appear composed as she picked up the coffee pot.

But, despite her best efforts, her hand trembled as she poured the liquid, and some of the coffee splashed onto the cloth. 'Oh, damn!' she muttered frustratedly. 'This is getting to be a habit. I'm sorry I'm so clumsy, Will. I don't know what's the matter with me this morning.'

Will resumed his own seat and regarded her wryly. 'Oh, I think you do,' he said steadily. 'After what you told me last night, I think you're bearing up very well.' He paused. 'But you're safe here, Francesca. You don't have to worry about any intruders. And the only things that are likely to follow you are the dogs.'

'I know.' Francesca managed a faint smile. 'Thanks.' She added cream to her coffee without accident and gave him a rueful look. 'And thanks for listening to me last night. I guess I just needed someone to talk to. I know it was a liberty coming here, but I think it's worked.'

'What's worked?' he enquired, his brows drawing together above eyes that were so dark, in some lights they looked black. He frowned. 'I haven't done anything except give you a bed for the night. You're not telling me that's made any conceivable difference to the situation?'

Francesca drew a breath. He was regarding her closely now, and she thought how much less intimidating he seemed this morning without his formal clothes. Tight-fitting jeans and a baggy sweater might not detract from his innate air of good breeding, but they did make him seem more approachable, she thought.

'I feel better because I've talked it out,' she explained firmly. 'I don't feel half so tense this morning, and I'm even prepared to admit that perhaps the situation isn't really as bad as I thought.'

Will's eyes narrowed. 'But your window was broken, wasn't it? He did make that call?'

'Oh, yes.' She flushed defensively. 'But he was probably only guessing about me finding the window. I mean—it could have been kids who broke it. He could have been using the fact that he'd seen it was broken to his own advantage.'

'Do you believe that?'

She moved her shoulders. 'It's an idea.' She hesitated. 'We do get some vandalism, too. Everybody does.'

'We?'

Once again, he questioned her use of the pronoun, and she gave him an indignant look. 'I meant as a general problem,' she declared, taking refuge in her coffee. But she sensed he was still suspicious of the situation. Perhaps he thought she was running away from an unhappy affair.

'I believe you said you'd reported the broken window to your landlady,' Will remarked now, and she nodded.

'Yes. She said she'd inform the police, and get her son-in-law to replace it.' She coloured. 'I didn't tell her about the phone call. It's not something I like to talk about.'

Will lay back in his chair, regarding her with a disturbing intensity, and she knew a desperate need to defend herself. 'I'm not lying,' she said. 'If you don't believe me, ring Mrs Bernstein. She'll confirm that the window was broken, and she'll be thrilled if you tell her who you are.'

Will's mouth flattened. 'I haven't said I don't believe you,' he responded, lifting his shoulders. 'On the contrary, I'm wondering what the hell I can do. There has to be some way to stop this bastard. Breaking and entering is still a crime, isn't it? It was the last time I checked.'

Francesca sighed, but before she could make any reply the elderly butler came into the room, carrying a tray. 'Good morning, madam,' he said, with rather more confidence than he'd shown the night before. 'I trust you slept well?'

'Very well, thank you, Watkins,' said Francesca, giving him a smile. It was good to know that Will's staff didn't hold their separation against her, and she flashed

Watkins a diffident look as he placed a rack of toast, a fresh dish of butter and a new pot of coffee beside her plate.

The butler departed, and although she wasn't particularly hungry Francesca helped herself to a piece of toast. Despite what she had told Will, she was not looking forward to going back to London, and her mouth dried at the thought of sleeping at the flat tonight.

'Well, isn't it?' Will prompted now, and she realised he was still waiting for a reply. 'Breaking and entering, I mean. You have to tell them what happened, Fran. It's something concrete they can work on.'

'Who? The police?' Francesca buttered the toast and then reached for the marmalade. Anything to buy herself a bit of time. 'You don't understand, Will. I can't prove who tried to get into the flat, can I? There are dozens—probably hundreds—of robberies every day. And as far as I could see nothing was stolen. So...'

Will's nostrils flared. 'But in the circumstances—'

Francesca shook her head. 'I'm not the only woman who's being harassed, Will. Like I said before, I probably overreacted. I just need to get myself together.'

He made a frustrated sound. 'I could kill him!'

'Yes, so could I,' she responded lightly, firmly lifting the toast to her lips. But her throat dried as she tried to swallow the tiny corner she'd nibbled, and she had to take a mouthful of coffee to enable her to get it down.

Will regarded her consideringly. 'So what are you going to do? When you get back, I mean. Would it help if you moved house?'

'And go and live with people I don't even know?' protested Francesca, putting the toast down again. 'Will, I've got to handle this. I can't go running scared every time he makes a move.'

Will's lips compressed. 'Okay,' he said. 'Okay, I can appreciate your feelings, but you've got to appreciate mine. Dammit, last night you were in a state of almost mental collapse. Forgive me if I find this sudden appearance of confidence hard to take.'

'I'm not confident.' Francesca couldn't let him think that. 'But I can't let him—let him beat me. After all, I can't prove he's committed any crime.'

'Apart from attempting to break into your apartment, and threatening you, you mean?' pointed out Will sardonically, and Francesca gave him a troubled look.

'I don't know if that was him,' she insisted, taking another mouthful of her coffee. And at his snort of disbelief she added, 'He's never broken a window before.'

'That's what worries me,' declared Will shortly. 'How do you know what the bastard will do next?'

Francesca sucked in a breath. 'Well, it's not your problem, is it?' she said, with determined brightness. 'And I am grateful to you for letting me stay here last night. I guess I just let the whole thing get on top of me. Which reminds me, would you mind if I rang my boss at Teniko, to explain that I might not make it into the office today?'

Will came forward in his chair. 'You can tell him you *won't* make it into the office today, if you like,' he asserted flatly. 'For God's sake, Fran, you don't think I'm going to let you drive back today? It's Friday, for pity's sake. I suggest you leave any heroics until Monday. Spend the weekend here at the Abbey. Don't worry; no one's going to touch you here, and at least it will give you a break.'

Francesca swallowed. 'You'd let me spend the weekend at the Abbey?' she exclaimed, and Will gave her an impatient look.

'Why not?' he asked. 'You look as if you could use the rest. At the least, it will give you time to think.'

'Maybe...' Francesca moistened her lips. 'But what will—what will Lady Rosemary have to say? It's the middle of the summer, so I assume she's staying at Mulberry Court. I don't think she'd approve of you offering to let me stay here.'

A frown brought his brows together at her words, and, judging by his expression, she suspected he hadn't given his grandmother's feelings a thought until then. But the old lady had always been a force to be reckoned with, and years ago Francesca had been left in no doubt that she was not the wife Lady Rosemary would have chosen for her grandson.

'This is my home,' he said, after a moment's consideration, but she had the feeling he was not as casual as he'd have her believe. Still, what the hell? she thought. There was no reason why she should meet the old lady. She'd just as soon that Will didn't tell her that she was here.

But, of course, someone was bound to. Even if she left today, her visit would not go unremarked. Watkins was an old gossip, and so was Mrs Harvey, and, although they were both extremely loyal to the family, when Francesca had left Will she'd forfeited any right to privacy.

'All the same...' she said now, giving him an out, but for reasons best known to himself Will chose not to take it.

'Please stay,' he said politely, though she thought his lips had stiffened. 'But I am expecting guests for lunch, so if you'll excuse me I have arrangements to make.'

CHAPTER FOUR

IT HAD been a reckless thing to do, and Will knew it. Allowing Francesca to stay the night at the Abbey was one thing; inviting her to spend the weekend there was something else.

At any other time, it wouldn't have mattered, he supposed. At any other time, he would not have been expecting a prospective 'fiancée' within a couple of hours. His grandmother was going to be furious, and with good reason, he reflected dourly. Apart from anything else, she'd be livid that Francesca should have come to him for help.

So why had he suggested Francesca should stay over until Sunday? It wasn't as if her being here was going to change the situation at all. Sooner or later she would have to go back, and face whatever it was that was waiting for her. It was just that she had looked so weary, somehow, so defeated. He hadn't had the heart to send her away.

Besides, after what she had told him, he needed a little more time to assimilate the information; to maybe think of some way he could help. It wasn't his problem, but she had been his wife and he felt a certain amount of responsibility for her. It was ridiculous perhaps—his grandmother was bound to think so—but sometimes it was necessary to put practical thoughts aside.

In any case, for the moment he had his own immediate future to think of, and he went in search of Mrs Harvey to ensure she was informed there were only *four* for lunch. He'd already made the arrangement, but after Watkins' treatment of Francesca he was wary. He could imagine how awkward they'd all feel if there were five places laid at the table.

If Mrs Harvey was surprised that his ex-wife was staying at the Abbey, she was shrewd enough not to show it. She left it to him to explain that *Ms* Quentin would be lunching in the morning room, and not in the dining room with him and his guests. He had considered suggesting that Francesca eat in her own rooms upstairs, but that smacked too much of subterfuge, and he assured himself he had nothing to hide.

Nevertheless, as he drove over to Mulberry Court later that morning, he realised he would have to inform his grandmother of his uninvited guest. He couldn't permit her to hear the news via one of the servants, and he was well aware that Lady Rosemary's maid was a frequent visitor at the Abbey.

Which was why he'd ensured that he arrived there fifteen minutes before the time he was expected. With a bit of luck, he'd find his grandmother alone, and he could explain why he'd allowed his ex-wife to stay on.

He should have known it wouldn't be that easy, he reflected, when, after parking at the front of the house, he sauntered into the hall. The door was standing ajar this morning to allow the sunlight to filter into the panelled foyer, and as soon as he stepped over the threshold Emma appeared on the half landing that divided the dog-leg staircase.

'Hello,' she said, with evident approval, and, resting one slim hand on the banister, she came prettily down the remaining stairs. 'You're early,' she added, clearly interpreting that as an indication of his enthusiasm to see her again. 'Mummy and Daddy are almost ready.' She gave a gurgling laugh. 'Well, Daddy is, anyway. Mummy's still deciding what she ought to wear.'

Will managed a smile, aware that Emma had obviously not had that problem herself. Her cream georgette blouse and matching shorts would have fitted her for almost any occasion, her silvery hair scooped back on one side with an ivory clip.

'As a matter of fact, I wanted a quick word with my grandmother,' he remarked, after offering a polite greeting, and Emma's expression tightened a little as she recognised her mistake. 'Do you know where she is?' he asked, glancing doubtfully about him. 'Is she in the orangery again? She spends a lot of her time in there.'

'I really couldn't say.' Emma spoke tersely at first, and then, as if realising she could hardly object to him wanting to speak to his grandmother, she recovered herself. 'I—she was reading the morning newspaper on the terrace,' she offered rather more warmly. 'I had breakfast with her, actually. Mummy and Daddy had theirs in their room.'

'Ah.'

Will reflected that he should have known. Lady Rosemary enjoyed eating her meals al fresco, and the terrace at the back of the house had a delightful view of the Vale of York in the distance.

'I'll come with you—if you don't mind, of course,' Emma said comfortably now, and Will realised there was nothing he could say to dissuade her. Short of being rude, that was. He sighed. But how could he explain about Francesca with Emma looking on?

Lady Rosemary was no less surprised to see him. 'Early, Will?' she exclaimed, putting her newspaper aside and tilting her cheek for his kiss. 'This is a first. You're obviously having a good influence on him, Emma. My grandson is notoriously unpunctual. As witness his late arrival yesterday evening.'

Will's expression was sardonic. 'You don't lose any opportunity to score a point, do you, Rosie?' he mocked. 'As a matter of fact, I had a reason.' He glanced meaningfully at Emma. 'Something has come up.'

'Has it?' Lady Rosemary frowned. 'Has it really? Does this mean you can't accommodate Emma and her parents for lunch?'

'I didn't say that,' said Will swiftly, aware of that young woman's eyes upon him. 'No—as a matter of fact, it's something else. It's a little—inconvenient, perhaps, but it's nothing I can't handle.'

His grandmother regarded him intently. 'It has to do with the Abbey, I assume.'

'In a manner of speaking,' replied Will, wondering if this had been such a good idea after all. Perhaps it would have been simpler just to let the old lady find out about Francesca. At least that way the lunch would have been over before she heard the news.

However, as if comprehending that whatever it was her grandson had to say it was not something he chose to discuss in front of Emma, Lady Rosemary turned her attention to the young woman in question. 'My dear,' she said, 'would you be a darling and ask Mrs Baxter if we could have some more coffee? I'm sure Will would like some, and perhaps you'd like a cup, too.'

'Of course.'

Emma was eager to do anything she could to aid the old lady, and, with an arching of her brows at Will, she turned back into the house. And as soon as she was gone Lady Rosemary looked enquiringly in Will's direction. 'You've got about three minutes, by my reckoning,' she said crisply. 'What's wrong?'

Will pushed his hands into the pockets of his dark blue trousers. He had changed out of the sweater and jeans he'd worn at breakfast into well-cut trousers and a silk shirt. 'It's Francesca,' he said, without preamble. 'She's at the Abbey. She arrived last night while I was having dinner here.'

His grandmother's air of calm authority vanished. 'Francesca!' she exclaimed disbelievingly. 'Francesca is here?'

'At Lingard,' agreed Will drily, pulling out a cane chair and straddling it. 'It's no problem really, but I thought you should hear the news from me and not somebody else.'

Lady Rosemary gasped. 'No problem, you say!' she cried incredulously. 'Will, are you mad? What's that woman doing here? And why haven't you sent her on her way?' Her eyes narrowed. 'You didn't invite her, did you?'

'Of course not.' Will rested muscled forearms along the back of the chair. 'I've told you, she arrived while I was here last evening.' He paused. 'She's—upset. I've said she can stay over the weekend.'

His grandmother's mouth mirrored her irritation. It was flattened and drawn into a thin line. 'I can't believe that, Will,' she said. 'I can't believe you've offered her your hospitality. Whatever is wrong with Francesca Goddard, then for God's sake let her deal with it herself.'

'It's not that simple.'

'Why isn't it?' Lady Rosemary's nostrils flared. 'Must I remind you, Will, this is the woman who aborted your unborn child? I don't care what's happened to her since she left Lingard. Whatever it is, it can't be any worse than the pain she put you through.'

Will sighed. 'That was a long time ago—'

'Not so long. And you're not going to try and tell me that she's changed, are you? The woman's poison, Will, and you know it. Get rid of her before she ruins your life yet again.'

Will heaved a breath. 'You're so bitter, Rosie.'

'I'm not bitter!' His grandmother was incensed. 'I'm just practical, that's all. And you should be, too. And don't call me Rosie,' she added irritably. 'Oh, Will, I thought you had more sense!'

Will's eyes had cooled considerably. 'I haven't forgotten the past, old lady,' he told her flatly, flicking an inquisitive insect off his wrist. His mouth twisted. 'I don't need you on my back, acting as my conscience. Whom I choose—or do not choose—to entertain at Lingard is my concern.'

Lady Rosemary drew in her lips, and he thought for a moment she was preparing for another attack. But then her face cleared, she fixed a false smile on her lips and, glancing over his shoulder, Will was not surprised to see Emma emerging from the house.

'Mrs Baxter says she'll bring it in a few minutes,' the young woman announced cheerfully, and, looking at his grandmother, Will realised she had no idea what Emma meant.

So, 'Good,' he applauded, rising politely to his feet. 'I think we could all use a cup of coffee, couldn't we, old lady?'

His grandmother gathered her composure quickly. 'Indeed we could,' she responded, as if she'd known what Emma was talking about all along. She hesitated, and then continued, 'Will was just telling me how much he's looking forward to taking you to Lingard, my dear.' She determinedly avoided her grandson's eyes as she went on, 'You're lucky. The Abbey grounds aren't open to the public until two o'clock today.'

'Is that right?'

Emma turned to Will now, and he was forced to explain the visiting arrangements at the Abbey to her. But when his eyes met his grandmother's over Emma's head she knew he wasn't relishing his role.

And despite the admiration he'd felt for Emma the night before Will wished with all his heart he could get out of the present situation. He felt like a fraud, suddenly, his unwilling concern for Francesca and her problems souring his mood.

Thankfully, Mrs Baxter came bustling out with the requested pot of coffee just then, and when Emma sat down Will resumed his previous position. And although in all honesty he didn't want anything else he forced himself to swallow several mouthfuls of the dark, aromatic beverage.

'Lady Rosemary was telling us that the gardens at Lingard Abbey are quite beautiful,' Emma said, after a moment. 'Mummy will love it. She's quite keen on horticulture and all that. She works very closely with our

gardener at home, and the house is always full of flow-
ers.'

'Really?'

Will didn't sound particularly interested, and his
grandmother made an exasperated sound. But when
Emma looked her way she turned it into a polite cough,
and then said, with obvious indulgence, 'I'm sure you
get much better weather in Cambridge than we do here.'

'Oh, I wouldn't say that.' Emma glanced diffidently
at Will. 'We're certainly having lovely weather at the
moment, aren't we?'

'We certainly are.' Will wondered how he had ever
got himself into this position. Then, with a determined
effort, he asked, 'What are your interests, Emma? What
do you do? I can't believe you find—earthy things so
fascinating.'

'It depends what earthy things you mean,' retorted
Emma, dimpling, obviously finding this comment more
to her taste. She bit her lip, casting a doubtful look in
Lady Rosemary's direction. 'I enjoy all sorts of things.
How about you?'

Will hesitated. 'What do I do in my spare time, do
you mean?' he asked, aware that his grandmother was
watching their exchange with rather more approval. 'I
enjoy sports—some sports, anyway; and I read a lot—
technical books, mostly. But since Lingard is under-
staffed, and my regular bailiff is recovering from a heart
attack, I spend most of my time these days ensuring that
the old place doesn't fall down.'

Emma caught her breath. 'You're joking.'

'About what?'

Emma looked to his grandmother for support.
'Lingard isn't likely to fall down, is it?'

'Not if I have anything to do with it,' declared Lady
Rosemary firmly. 'Don't take any notice of my grandson, my dear. He's teasing you, that's all.'

'Am I?'

Will regarded the old lady with an accusing gaze, and

she impatiently thrust her coffee cup onto the glass-topped table. 'Indeed you are, Will,' she assured him crisply. 'The Abbey will be there long after you and I are dead and gone. You know perfectly well how important it is to preserve these old buildings—for posterity, if nothing else.'

'If you say so, old lady,' Will responded carelessly, realising there was no point in starting that kind of argument at present. Besides, he'd agreed to meet the Merritts. His grandmother hadn't forced him. Even if the underlying theme to all Lady Rosemary's remarks was to remind him of his responsibilities.

'What kind of sports do you like?' Emma interposed now, evidently deciding that she'd been out of the conversation long enough. 'I bet you play polo,' she added, watching him slyly. 'You look as if you do. Polo players have to have strong shoulders and powerful thighs.'

'Emma!'

Her mother's horrified exclamation saved Will from having to answer that. Instead, he exchanged a mocking look with his grandmother who for once chose not to meet it with reproof. On the contrary, he could see Lady Rosemary was as taken aback by Emma's audacity as he was, and Lady Merritt hurried to make amends.

'I must apologise for my daughter, Lady Rosemary!' she exclaimed, giving the young woman an impatient stare. 'I don't know what the world's coming to. These days girls think they can say whatever they like.'

'Well, I—'

Lady Rosemary started to speak, but once again Emma chose to have her say. 'Oh, don't be so old-fashioned, Mummy,' she declared. 'Will's not embarrassed, are you?' She bestowed another provocative glance in his direction. 'You do play polo, don't you? I can always tell.'

Will was getting up from his chair as she spoke, and he allowed Lady Merritt an apologetic smile. 'I'm afraid I have to disappoint you,' he replied as Sir George followed his wife onto the terrace. 'The only team game I've ever played is rugby. I guess I'm more of a spectator these days.'

Emma pouted, but happily her father seemed to have more sway than her mother. 'Emma's spoilt,' he said addressing no one in particular. 'The youths she usually runs around with think it's clever to be rude.'

'Oh, Daddy!' Emma's jaw dropped. 'You make me sound like a kid who's scarcely out of the schoolroom. I am eighteen, you know, not eight. If men can speak their minds, why shouldn't women have the same privilege?'

'Because they can't,' said her mother firmly, as if that was the end of it. She turned to Will. 'I'm sorry if George and I have kept you waiting. I was sure you said a quarter to.'

'I did.' Will flexed his hands on the back of his chair. 'I was early.' He met his grandmother's gaze. 'I guess we'd better be on our way.'

Lady Rosemary got up now, compelling Emma to do the same, and regarded her grandson with obvious unease. 'You will—let me know what happens—about the—about the difficulty you mentioned,' she ventured awkwardly, and Will nodded.

'I'll be in touch later,' he agreed, shepherding his guests into the house. 'The car's out front,' he added, in answer to Sir George's enquiry. 'You'll have to forgive me if it's dusty. We haven't had any rain for several weeks.'

'Will!'

He was guiding the Merritts out of the front entrance when he heard his grandmother calling his name. With a word of apology to the others, he bid them get into the Range Rover, and came back.

'What now?'

Lady Rosemary sighed. 'You never did tell me what Francesca wants,' she said stiffly, clearly not appreciating his impatience. 'I assume she does want something.

There wouldn't be much point in her coming here otherwise.'

Will hooked his thumbs into the pockets of his trousers. 'She doesn't *want* anything,' he said at last. 'Nothing tangible, that is. I can't discuss it now, old lady. Your guests—*my* guests—will be getting impatient.'

Lady Rosemary's lips tightened. 'You delight in annoying me, don't you, Will? At least have the goodness to tell me you don't intend to introduce her to the Merritts.'

'I don't,' said Will flatly. 'Now, can I go? I'll speak to you later today. After I've done my duty.'

CHAPTER FIVE

FRANCESCA heard the sound of voices as she was adding a touch of blusher to her pale cheeks.

She'd decided to go down to the village. If she was to stay for the weekend, there were certain things she needed, and she remembered from when she'd lived here that the stores in the village could supply most of what she desired.

But the sound of feminine laughter drew her to the windows, and, looking out, she saw Will, another man and two women sauntering casually through the Abbey gardens.

His guests for lunch, she perceived, aware of an unwarranted sense of trespass. But this wasn't her home any longer, and she had no right to feel aggrieved because Will had invited some other women here. Nevertheless, she wondered who they were and what they were doing here. She sensed, in spite of their amicability with one another, that they were not familiar with the Abbey grounds.

She watched them for a few minutes more, and then, feeling like a voyeur, she moved away from the windows. It wasn't anything to do with her, she told herself, annoyed that she was even interested. But the younger woman was pretty, and Will seemed incapable of taking his eyes off her.

She had applied some lipstick, and now she circled her lips with her tongue, tasting the oily cosmetic, examining the texture of her skin with a critical eye. These last few months had exacted a toll upon her. She couldn't look at herself now without seeing herself through someone else's eyes.

And, as always, the memory of what had brought her here sent a cold shiver down her spine. Any resentment she might have been feeling at the evidence that Will was getting on with his life was quickly dissipated. Instead of thinking about Will, she should be thinking about her future, she thought tremulously. Not least, what she was going to do when she went home.

Home.

Her skin prickled in protest. Home was supposed to be a safe place. She couldn't imagine that her apartment would ever feel safe again. Not so long as *he* was out there. Her hand shook uncontrollably. Oh, God, what was she going to do?

A choking feeling assailed her, and she took several deep breaths to control herself. This was ridiculous, she told herself severely. Was she going to let this—this moron ruin her life? Whoever he was, he was sick. No one in their right mind would get their kicks from frightening someone half to death. Somehow, she had to deal with this. It was her problem, no one else's. She swallowed. Least of all Will's.

The voices seemed louder and, giving in to the urge to find out what was happening, she edged closer to the window again. But this time she kept the width of the curtain between herself and possible detection. The last thing she wanted was for Will to think she was spying on him. She grimaced. Even if she was.

Will and his party were climbing the steps to the terrace when she ventured to peer through the wavy glass again. They had apparently been nearing the end of their tour when she'd first detected their presence, and now, after admiring the beauties of the lake and the water gardens, they were returning to the house for lunch.

She could see now that one of the two women was much older than the other. She must be well into her forties, or even her early fifties, perhaps. It was difficult to be certain from such a distance away. And the other man was of a similar age, which pointed to the fact that they were a couple. Which meant that the younger woman was Will's partner, as she'd half suspected before.

She caught her lower lip between her teeth as Will and the young woman followed the older couple up the stone flagged steps. Whoever she was, she was beautiful, acknowledged Francesca, with a rueful sigh. And she was also flirting with her partner, turning her face up to his, and occasionally pretending to need his arm for support. It was obvious she'd have been quite content if they'd been alone together. When the older woman turned to speak to her, her face took on a slightly sullen pout.

Francesca thought Will looked a little thoughtful, but perhaps that was just wishful thinking. *Wishful thinking?* She was appalled at the connotation. It didn't matter to her who Will chose to get involved with. He was a free man, after all, and still young enough to start all over again.

As she should have done, thought Francesca painfully, drawing back to rest her shoulders against the heavily patterned damask that covered the walls of the bedroom. If she'd found someone else, got married again, she wouldn't be in this position now. The trouble was, her experience with Will had made her wary. She didn't know if she'd ever trust a man with her future again.

Yet it had taken a long time to get Will out of her system. Even though she had been reeling from the shock of his accusation, she had still been unable to believe that what they had was over. She couldn't accept it, couldn't believe what had happened to her. For a time, she'd existed in a kind of vacuum, convinced that sooner or later Will would realise his mistake.

He hadn't. Seemingly, he'd been quite prepared to believe the worst of her—and all because she had hinted that she might go back to work after the baby was born. He apparently couldn't—or wouldn't—understand that that didn't mean her home and family meant any less to her. He had always got Lingard; why couldn't he see that she needed some independence, too?

Still, that was all water under the bridge now, she reflected ruefully. Her pregnancy hadn't lasted long enough for the whys and wherefores of returning to work afterwards to become a problem. When she'd expected Will's sympathy, she'd been denied it; instead, she'd been accused of gross selfishness and betrayal, of putting her needs before those of anyone else.

She was getting maudlin. She could feel the tears pricking at the back of her eyes, and she was appalled at her own weakness. For heaven's sake, she hadn't come here to indulge in mawkish sentiment. If Will had been so willing to think the worst of her, it was better that she'd found out when she had.

She straightened, pulling a tissue out of the box on the dressing table and dabbing carefully at the skin beneath her eyes. All she needed now was for her mascara to draw even blacker lines around her eyes, she thought cynically. Seeing Will's—new?—girlfriend had aroused old memories, that was all.

She glanced down at her jeans and shirt, wondering if she ought to change before venturing into the village. If she thought there was any chance that Will's guests might see her, she would definitely put on more formal clothes. Or would she? Francesca bit her lip. What did her appearance matter? It wasn't as if Will would be eager to introduce her to his guests.

She started towards the door, and then halted uncertainly. Was it wise for her to leave the Abbey while those people were here? She had no desire to meet them, no desire to be accused of snooping. Perhaps she should wait until they'd left before making her presence so obvious. She couldn't be sure they wouldn't hear the car, and ask Will who she was.

Her lips twitched involuntarily. There was a certain amount of amusement to be gained from picturing Will's embarrassment if he had to explain. She wondered what excuse he'd offer for his ex-wife to be staying at the Abbey. The truth might not be to his liking if he was hoping to marry again.

A knock at the door didn't cause quite the same terror as it had done the night before, but she nevertheless turned to answer the summons with some reluctance. She hoped Will hadn't changed his mind, and decided to invite her to join them. Although the prospect caused ripples of anticipation, common sense warned her not to get involved again.

It was Mrs Harvey who had knocked at the door, and the housekeeper regarded Francesca with obvious discomfort. 'I—er—I've come to ask you when you'd like to eat, Mrs Quentin,' she declared, looking a little flustered. 'I've laid the table in the morning room, like his lordship suggested.'

Francesca refused to acknowledge the hollowing in her stomach at the housekeeper's words, and, realising that Mrs Harvey was as unhappy with the arrangements as she was, she said gently, 'Couldn't I just have a tray? I'm really not very hungry, I'm afraid.'

'A tray?' Mrs Harvey looked a little more enthusiastic. 'Well, yes,' she said at once. 'Of course you can have a tray, if you'd prefer it. Only his lordship said you'd want to eat downstairs.'

'Well, I'd rather not,' said Francesca firmly, realising she could fill in the time until Will's guests left making a couple of calls. She'd promised Clare she would ring, and Tom Radley would probably be worried about her, too. She hoped Clare had found the time to explain to him where she was. She doubted her boss at Teniko, whom she had phoned earlier that morning, would have informed him that she wouldn't be in today.

Of course, she hadn't told Mr Hamishito where she was or what was happening. The less her employer knew about the situation the better. She had the feeling Mr Hamishito might consider she was to blame in some way for encouraging the stalker. She'd already sensed that the vice-president of Teniko considered women an inferior breed.

'If you're sure,' Mrs Harvey said now, and Francesca assured her that she was.

'Just a light lunch, please,' she added apologetically. 'I usually just have a sandwich at midday.'

Mrs Harvey departed, but not before she'd given Francesca a look which seemed to imply that neglecting herself was a mistake. Francesca pulled a wry face as she closed the door. The housekeeper was probably right; she could do with gaining a little weight. But since *he* had started following her she hadn't had much interest in food.

Clare was at her desk when she rang, as Francesca had hoped she'd be, and she expressed some relief at hearing from her friend. 'I was beginning to get worried,' she said. 'I thought you were going to phone Hamishito.'

'I was. I did,' said Francesca quickly. 'I assume he hasn't mentioned the fact that I'm supposed to be ill?'

'Not a word,' said Clare firmly. 'Though I should have known he must have heard something when he didn't ask where you were. So...' She waited. 'How are you? Did your ex-husband let you stay?'

'Yes.' Francesca sighed, and then added reluctantly, 'He says I can spend the weekend, if I want. I am tempted, but can you manage without your car?' She paused. 'Of course you have my spare set of keys. You could always use my car if you were stuck.'

'No problem.' Clare was adamant. 'If I want to go anywhere, I'll get Mick to take me. Besides...' she paused '...it's not as if he uses his car at weekends. So long as there's football on the telly, he won't move an inch.'

Francesca smiled. Since Clare's husband had lost his job, he was inclined to be a couch potato, though he would not have liked anyone to say so. To combat his enforced idleness, he was also a member of a gym, and he worked out there several times a week.

'Well—okay,' said Francesca. 'And thanks.' She bit her lip. 'For being so understanding last night.' As with her landlady, she hadn't mentioned the phone call to Clare. It had been enough to say that someone had tried to break in.

'Hey, what are friends for?' exclaimed Clare, her voice warm and reassuring. 'If there's anything else I can do, just let me know.'

It was harder phoning Tom Radley. As she had expected, he knew nothing of what had transpired the night before. It meant Francesca had to tell him where she was before she could get around to explaining about the broken window, and Tom was instantly offended because she hadn't contacted him.

'I've told you I'm willing to stay at the flat until this pervert gets tired and finds someone else to annoy!' he exclaimed angrily. 'There was no need for you to go haring off to Yorkshire.' He paused. 'Besides, I didn't think you and your ex-husband were on such friendly terms.'

'We're not.' Francesca tried to placate him. 'But try and understand my feelings, Tom. Getting home and finding someone had tried to get into the flat was bad enough, but knowing that—that it was *him*—'

'Was anything stolen?'

Francesca gasped. 'I—why—I don't think so.'

'You don't think so?' Tom sounded incredulous. 'Francesca, surely that was the first thing you should have checked.'

After getting that call! Oh, sure.

Francesca swallowed. 'I—suppose I never thought about it,' she answered honestly. 'I was—upset.'

'Even so.' Tom was insistent. 'If he's stolen something, it would prove to the police that he'd really been there.' He hesitated. 'Perhaps you should have checked your underwear. I believe that's the kind of thing they usually go for.'

Francesca caught her breath. 'Tom!'

'Well…' He had the grace to sound a little shame-faced now. 'I'm just trying to be practical, Francesca. You've read about men like this before, surely?'

Francesca sighed. 'All right. I'm fairly sure nothing had been touched. But it was an awful feeling, Tom. A sort of creepy feeling, knowing he might possibly have been in the flat. All I could think about was getting out of there. Clare said I could stay with her and Mick, but I just wanted to get away.'

'To Yorkshire!'

'To anywhere.' Francesca could feel a shred of resentment stirring in her now. 'Tom, please try and understand. I was frightened. This—this man doesn't just—annoy me; he scares me stiff.'

There was silence for a moment, and then, when Tom spoke again, there was considerably less animosity in his tone. 'Oh, very well,' he said. 'If it works for you, then who am I to argue? But when you get back you're going to have to make some more permanent arrangement.'

Francesca agreed, as much because it was expedient to do so as for any real conviction on her part. The unpalatable truth was, she didn't have any idea how to handle this, and despite his concern she couldn't see herself letting Tom set up home in her living room.

She rang off, promising to speak to him when she got back on Monday, and by then a maid she didn't recognise was knocking at her door with her lunch. It reminded her that Mrs Harvey probably had more important things to do than attend to her needs, and that her previous concern had more to do with curiosity than anything else.

Even so, she couldn't help being impressed by the meal that was provided. Instead of a tray, the maid wheeled a serving trolley into the room, swinging out the sides and spreading the cloth with great ceremony. As well as the salad Francesca had expected, there was a cold soup and lamb cutlets, with a raspberry summer pudding to finish.

And, despite her contention that she wasn't hungry, Francesca found herself enjoying the food. The asparagus soup was light and creamy, the lamb cutlets, served with a mint jelly, were crisp and tasty, and the raspberry pudding just melted in her mouth.

So much for not having an appetite, she reflected as she poured herself a cup of coffee from the jug she'd found residing on one of the lower shelves. And, in spite of a lingering stab of anxiety, caused as much by her phone call to Tom Radley as anything else, she felt infinitely better with the food inside her.

She doubted Will and his guests could have had a nicer meal, and thinking of Will reminded her that she still hadn't been into the village. She glanced at her watch. It was half past one, and she wondered how long his guests were staying. It would be annoying if they remained until teatime. She doubted that the shops in Lingard village would stay open after five.

She retouched her make-up, checked that her hair was still neat, and then stood restlessly by the windows. Could she possibly leave the Abbey without anyone noticing? Perhaps if she waited until after two o'clock she could mingle with the visitors and leave that way. The trouble was, she wasn't absolutely sure where they'd put her—Clare's—car. Watkins had asked her for the keys earlier that morning, in order that it could be moved to the garage block.

She sighed. Will's orders, no doubt. He wouldn't want the jaunty little sports car left on display for everyone to see. Apart from anything else, it would have been bound to provoke too many questions. He might be prepared to tell his grandmother she was here, but she doubted he'd want to explain his actions to anyone else.

She frowned. She could always walk to the village,

of course. It wasn't that far—a couple of miles at most. Less, if she used the old bridle-way that came out by the churchyard. The green was immediately opposite the church, with the shops, such as they were, screened by a small beck and a row of poplars beyond that.

It was better than cooling her heels here for another hour, she decided, scanning the sky for any sign of rain. But the afternoon was fine, the sky almost completely clear of any clouds, and she was eager to get out of doors and get some air.

The recollection that there was a secondary staircase that wound down into the service hall was the decisive factor. Years ago, it had also been used as a convenient means of reaching the nurseries on the second floor. Families had been much bigger in those days, and the staff hadn't asked for such high wages. Francesca remembered Will had told her that a dozen servants had slept up there as well.

Still, as far as she knew, no one occupied the second floor these days, and she felt confident she could leave the house that way without encountering any of Will's guests. They were probably enjoying after-lunch drinks in the drawing room. The imminent arrival of sightseers would prevent them from sitting outdoors.

Gathering up the strap of her bag, she looped it over her shoulder, and opened the bedroom door. She was tempted to wheel the trolley outside before she left, but that smacked too much of treating the place like a hotel, and instead she left dealing with it for later. Closing the door again, she walked swiftly along the passageway, finding her way to the nursery stairs without incident.

She had started down the stairs before she realised that someone was coming up. When she'd first heard the voices, she'd imagined they were coming from the hall below. She'd realised it was a man's voice interspersed with that of a woman, and assumed it was Watkins and one of the maids, or perhaps even Mrs Harvey. By the

time the tones were recognisable, it was too late to rec-
tify her mistake.

She could have backtracked, she supposed. It
wouldn't really have been all that difficult to scoot back
up the stairs until they were gone. But by the time she
had considered the alternatives the woman had rounded
the corner of the stairs and seen her; and by then it was
too late.

The woman got a shock; there was no other word for
it. Perhaps Will, who was following her, had been re-
galing her with some of the old myths and legends connected with the Abbey. It was certainly true that the
family had always fostered the belief that the place was
haunted, and when Francesca suddenly appeared before
her the young woman certainly looked as if she'd been
confronted by a ghost.

'My God!' she said, backing a step, and colliding with
Will's broad chest behind her. She swallowed. 'Damn,
you startled me!' She twisted round to look at Will. 'I
thought you said the servants didn't sleep upstairs any
more.'

'They don't.' Will's expression as he looked at
Francesca was not encouraging.

'Then—'

'I'm—just a friend of the family,' said Francesca
hastily, scurrying past them. 'Hello, Will. I'm just going
down to the village. I expect I'll see you later.'

CHAPTER SIX

WILL drove the Merritts back to Mulberry Court in the late afternoon.

He thought it had been a fairly successful visit, even if they had stayed rather longer than he had anticipated. But Emma had insisted on a guided tour of the Abbey, and although he had managed to avoid the private apartments she had expressed an interest in the old nurseries, and the attics, which she was sure, she'd told him romantically, were filled with an interesting record of his family history.

Rubbish, was what Will usually called the motley collection of broken and discarded furniture, Victorian steamer trunks, photograph albums, and boxes of memorabilia that crammed the dusty space beneath the roof. It was hot up there, and far too cloistered, but after that awkward encounter on the stairs he had been eager to do anything to put that particular incident out of her head.

There had been one difficult moment, after Francesca had gone on down the stairs, leaving him to face Emma's questions. But 'Why didn't your friend join us for lunch?' had been, in the end, quickly dealt with.

'She's just up from London for the weekend,' he'd said, glad he hadn't been obliged to make any introduction. 'She's—er—suffering something of a crisis, I believe. She came here to get away from it all.'

Thankfully, that had seemed to satisfy her—for the present, at least. Will suspected she was too sure of herself, and of her own beauty, to see anything remotely threatening about a woman of his own age, particularly at the moment, when Francesca's face looked pale and drawn. Besides, Emma didn't know him well enough yet to question who he invited to the Abbey. And, so long as she had his undivided attention, she was quite happy to dismiss the other woman from her mind.

Her parents, who had spent the time he was showing Emma around the Abbey enjoying a relaxing drink in the library, had evidently enjoyed their visit, too. He doubted they had needed their daughter's coy remarks about what fun they'd had exploring the attics and how exciting she'd found the old building to endorse their original opinion. As far as the Merritts were concerned, Lingard Abbey—and its owner—had something they desired: a title for their only daughter, and the kind of connections money couldn't buy.

Well, only indirectly, conceded Will cynically, aware that the Merritt millions would solve a lot, not to say all of his problems. A new roof and complete restoration of the stonework would do for starters, but there were a hundred and one other repairs that needed early—if not immediate—attention.

'Will we see you again before we leave?' asked Lady Merritt when they reached Mulberry Court, accepting the hand Will offered to help her down from the Range Rover, proving that so far as she was concerned she saw no point in standing on ceremony. He thought Sir George winced a little at his wife's lack of discretion, but Emma, following her mother out of the vehicle, was quick to offer a reply.

'Of course we will, Mummy!' she exclaimed, giving Will a conspiratorial smile. 'Will's promised to take me to York tomorrow. You'll see him when he comes to pick me up.'

'Is this true?'

Lady Merritt turned to Will now, and he was forced to concede that he had indeed mentioned that the city was worth a visit. That he hadn't actually made a definite arrangement with Emma was not something he chose to argue with at this moment. He had no reason not to fall in with her plans, after all. Not if he was even considering going ahead with his grandmother's scheme.

'Perhaps we could all go to York together,' Lady Merritt suggested eagerly, but Emma was having none of that.

'And leave Lady Rosemary on her own again?' she exclaimed, as if that were the real reason she was making a protest.

'Oh, well. Perhaps not,' murmured Lady Merritt, catching her husband's warning eye. 'In any case, thank you so much for lunch, and the tour of the gardens. I can't remember when I've enjoyed myself so much.'

They all went into the house together, Will feeling obliged to at least report to his grandmother before leaving again. But, for all he had promised to discuss Francesca's visit in more detail with the old lady later, he was not displeased to find she had had another visitor in their absence.

Archie Rossiter was seated with Lady Rosemary in the drawing room, the tray of tea between them an indication of how long he had been there. The old man rose politely to his feet as Lady Rosemary's other guests came into the room, shaking Sir George's hand, and complimenting Lady Merritt on the obvious benefits a stay in the country had had upon her appearance.

He smiled rather diffidently at Will, but the younger man was only too pleased not to have to face a catechism from his grandmother. Nevertheless, he was surprised that Archie was here again after having joined the party for dinner the evening before, and he wondered if he had overlooked the fact that the two old people had more in common than he'd thought.

'Did—er—did you have a pleasant afternoon?' enquired Lady Rosemary, speaking to the company in general, but seeking her grandson's cool dark gaze. It was obvious what she meant, but Will didn't feel inclined to humour her. For some reason, he was feeling particularly out of humour with her at this moment.

'Oh, we had a lovely time,' declared Emma, once again answering for him, and he wondered if this was the source of his present feeling of irritation. 'The gardens were beautiful, but I liked the house better. Will took me up into the attics and showed me all the old photograph albums and stuff like that.'

'Not *all* the old photograph albums, surely?' protested the old lady stiffly, and Will guessed she was wondering if he'd shown Emma any pictures of his first wife.

'There were too many!' exclaimed Emma, inadvertently reassuring her. 'But it was lots of fun all the same.' She flashed a teasing look at Will. 'Your grandson's such an interesting man, Lady Rosemary. Even if he doesn't play polo.'

'I'm sure.' The old lady managed a tight smile, and then reached for the bell-rope. 'You'll join us for tea, Will? Archie was just leaving.'

'I don't think so.' Will had had quite enough of the Merritts for one day. It wasn't that he didn't like Emma, he told himself. It was just that accepting what his grandmother expected of him wasn't getting any easier to swallow.

'Then I'll see you out,' said Lady Rosemary firmly, this time preventing any attempt on Emma's part to intervene. 'Just tell Mabel what you want,' she directed her guests pleasantly. 'Archie, you'll stay on for a moment, won't you? I just want to ask Will about his bailiff.'

They had left the room and were crossing the panelled hall when Will remarked casually, 'Actually Fielding's getting on very well. Since he had the operation, he's gone from strength to strength, and I know he's hoping to get back to work before the end of the summer.'

'Really?' Lady Rosemary did not sound particularly interested and, meeting her steely gaze, Will was not surprised to see the flash of anger in her eyes. 'Will, you know very well that I did not accompany you out here to hear about Maurice Fielding's heart attack. I want to know why Francesca Goddard is here, and why you permitted her to stay.'

Will sighed. 'As I said earlier, she's got a problem. Some—man is pestering her,' he admitted at last, and his grandmother made an exasperated sound.

'And you consider that sufficient reason to jeopardise your own future?' She shook her head. 'You baffle me, Will. You really do.'

Will shrugged. 'I didn't promise you'd like my explanation,' he said mildly. 'Anyway, it doesn't affect my dealings with the Merritts, if that's what you're afraid of. Emma met her today, but—'

Lady Rosemary caught her breath.

'—Francesca passed herself off as a friend of the family. And, to your relief, I'm sure, Emma is too conceited to imagine I might be more closely associated with her.'

The old lady was appalled nonetheless. 'Francesca met Emma?' she echoed, in horrified fascination. 'Will, you didn't invite that woman to join you for lunch? Not after what you said?'

'No, I didn't.' Will was getting impatient now, aware that the longer the old lady detained him, the greater the chance that Emma herself might come to see what was going on. 'I told you, she met Emma, not all the Merritts. We—Emma and I—ran into her by accident. Be thankful Francesca was tactful. She could have told her who she was.'

His grandmother sniffed. 'Are you so sure she won't?' she snapped, and Will couldn't help wondering why the old lady was so antagonistic towards his ex-wife. Was it only because of what she viewed as Francesca's betrayal, or did she know something about her that even he didn't know?

The possibilities were endless, and not wholly justifiable. It was true Francesca had aborted their child, and he'd never forgiven her for that. Indeed, every time he thought about it he got a bitter ache in his stomach. But so far as he knew she had never been unfaithful to him, and it was he, and not his grandmother, who had had to bear the pain.

'Look, I've got to go,' he said now, finding the connotations of this conversation too unpleasant to prolong. 'I've invited her to spend the weekend at Lingard, but that's all. I felt sorry for her, right? I'd have felt the same about any woman being hounded by some thug.'

'Well, if you're sure...'

'I am sure.' Will crossed the porch and went down the steps to where the Range Rover was waiting. 'I'll see you tomorrow. I've apparently promised to take Emma on a trip to York.'

Will drove back to the Abbey with the image of his grandmother's obvious delight at this news in the forefront of his mind. If only the old lady wasn't so desperate suddenly for a great-grandchild, he reflected broodingly, he wouldn't feel so pressured now. It wasn't as if she had always felt this way—or if she had she had hidden her feelings from him. He and Francesca had been together for over six years, and he couldn't remember his grandmother urging him to start a family at that time. On the contrary, she'd been firmly convinced that the marriage wouldn't last, and when she'd been proved right she'd been the first to offer the opinion that it was just as well there were no children involved.

He scowled. Why hadn't he realised before now just how much the old lady disliked his ex-wife? His mouth compressed. Probably because when he and Francesca had been together they hadn't spent a lot of time at Mulberry Court. The Abbey had always required a lot of his time, and Francesca had been working in Leeds, which meant that the time they had spent together was precious—too precious to spend with an old lady who spent half her time in London, and who, when she was in Yorkshire, usually disapproved of how they lived.

The silhouette of the Abbey appeared across the fields at that moment, the slight rise of land that formed its backdrop giving it an air of mystery in the mellow light. It was a beautiful sight, and he loved it, but he wondered if it was really worth the sacrifice of his freedom.

It was a warm evening, with the underlying threat of thunder hanging in the still air. Despite himself, he couldn't help wondering how Francesca had spent the afternoon, and whether she had really been heading for the village when they'd passed her on the stairs.

As usual, Watkins had heard the car and met him in the hall. There was no fire burning in the huge grate this evening, for which Will was grateful, and he forced his own concerns aside and gave the elderly butler a wry smile.

'Everything okay?' he asked, almost rhetorically, on his way to the library and the large Scotch he'd promised himself, and the old man asked, rather diffidently, if he knew where Mrs Quentin might be.

'Francesca?' Will swung round with a frown, annoyed to feel the jolt of anxiety that gripped his gut. 'What do you mean, do I know where she is? I assume she's in her room. Where else?'

'I'm afraid she's not there, my lord,' murmured Watkins, looking rather discomfited now. 'Edna tried to serve her afternoon tea about an hour ago, but she could get no reply. Then, later on, Mrs Harvey went to speak to her, but although she took the liberty of going into madam's room she said there was no sign of her.'

Will controlled his breathing with an effort. 'Well, she did go out earlier, didn't she?'

'Did she, my lord?'

'Yes.' Will could feel his anxiety increasing. 'I believe she went down to the village. Hasn't her car come back?'

'She didn't take her car, my lord. It's still in the garage. As you know, I had Smedley remove the car to the garage this morning and, according to him, it's still there.'

Will tried to keep things in perspective. Just because

Francesca had gone out about four hours ago and not returned, that was no reason to get into a panic. No one knew she was here—no one who might harm her, that was. The idea that she might have gone for a walk and been set upon by her stalker was just too incredible to be true. Yet the fact remained that she had been gone an awfully long time. What the hell was she doing, for God's sake? Didn't she realise he was bound to think the worst?

Calming himself, he said, 'Did no one see her go out?'

'None of the household staff, certainly, my lord.'

'I see.' Will could feel his nerves tightening in spite of himself. 'Then I suppose I'd better go and look for her. I'll take the Range Rover. It'll be quicker.'

'I'm sure it's nothing to worry about, my lord.' Now that he'd delivered his news, Watkins was at pains to assure him that nothing was wrong. 'Would you like myself or Smedley to accompany you? It's possible Mrs Quentin has lost her way.'

Will gave him a retiring look. 'I think not,' he declared crisply, remembering the years Francesca had spent at Lingard with some reluctance. 'It's all right, Watkins. I'll go alone. If she gets back before I do, you can ring me on the mobile phone.'

'Yes, my lord.'

Watkins still looked troubled, however, and Will was aware the old man took his duties of care very seriously. So far as the butler was concerned, it was his responsibility to ensure that all the guests at the Abbey were well and accounted for, and Francesca's disappearance was a source of anxiety to him.

Will was still brooding on this when he climbed behind the wheel of his car. How could Francesca have left the Abbey without telling anyone else she was going out? Particularly if she'd planned to stay out so long. It was thoughtless, and it was selfish, but he didn't really know why he should feel surprised. Francesca had always been thoughtless and selfish, hadn't she? Wasn't that what his grandmother had been trying to tell him less than an hour ago?

His breath escaped on an angry curse and, swinging the vehicle around, he drove rather recklessly down the drive, scattering the last few departing visitors as he went. He should leave her to come back when she was good and ready, he told himself grimly. Why should he care if she was safe or not?

Beyond the famous cultivated gardens that surrounded the Abbey, there were fields, and white-railed paddocks, where mares and geldings, and a few small ponies, grazed the grassy slopes that ran down to the River Linn. Will still owned the land, but he leased the paddocks to the nearby riding school, and in winter one of the local farmers bred his ewes in the fields beyond the spinney.

It was approximately two miles to the village by road, the twisting route narrowed still further by high hedges, at present in full leaf. Will could smell the scent of hawthorn blossom and the richer scent of newly turned soil, could see flocks of birds settling in the furrows as the tractor wound its way back to the farmer's yard. It was an idyllic scene, he reflected—the kind of image conjured up by expatriates when they were abroad. It was a pity he couldn't enjoy it, he thought bitterly, couldn't see beyond the sight of Francesca's bludgeoned body, bundled into a ditch.

He was crazy, he told himself fiercely. She'd met someone she knew, that was all. Someone she knew from the days when she'd lived at the Abbey, and with whom she'd struck up a conversation and forgotten the time. That had to be the solution. Anything else was purely make-believe.

At a quarter to six on a Friday afternoon the village was virtually deserted. There was the odd car about, and several were parked outside the George and Dragon, but most commuters were already home. Even the shops seemed singularly empty, and Will's fingers tightened on the wheel as he realised he was unlikely to find her here.

But then where?

He parked on the double yellow lines that edged the village green with a scant regard for authority, staring grimly about him. Then, pushing open his door, he got out and strode across the turf to the post office.

Mrs Simpson, who was the postmistress, and also one of the worst gossips in the village, eyed him with interest as he entered the shop. She sold sweets and tobacco too, but he was not a regular customer, and although he'd been about to ask for her help he changed his mind and requested a small box of cigars instead.

She knew who he was, of course, and he wondered, when she showed him the three brands she had for sale, if she imagined he smoked the things himself. Still, they'd do for Watkins, he decided irritably. At least he wouldn't have the ignominy of knowing that his affairs were being broadcast around the neighbourhood.

He chose the brand of cigars he wanted, and Mrs Simpson accepted the note he gave her with a friendly smile. 'Isn't it a lovely evening, my lord?' she remarked, perhaps hoping for a protracted conversation. 'We should enjoy them. It'll be autumn soon, and then the nights start drawing in.'

'I'm sure.'

Will was polite but noncommittal, wishing now he'd never gone into the post office in the first place. It was obvious Mrs Simpson was curious to know what he was doing in the village, and he doubted she believed he was there just to buy cigars.

'Your wife—that is, your ex-wife—was in earlier,' she offered as Will made for the door, and he endeavoured not to reveal any especial interest in her words.

'She was?' he said carelessly, and Mrs Simpson nodded.

'Yes. I was surprised to see her, too. She must be staying around these parts.'

She was waiting for him to confirm it, but Will couldn't do it. Not without betraying the fact that he might be checking up on her. Besides, he'd learned what he wanted to know: Francesca had come to the village. Which meant she must still be here. Either that, or on her way home.

Home! His lips twisted as he said good evening to a disappointed Mrs Simpson, and stepped out onto the pavement in front of the shop. The Abbey was not home to Francesca now. He had sometimes wondered if it ever had been. She had obviously always had her own agenda, which had not included being a mother to his children.

He took a deep breath. Mulling over old wounds was not going to help him now. And, as it seemed obvious that he was overreacting to Francesca's absence, the best thing he could do was go back to the Abbey. She'd turn up—when it suited her to do so. Until then, he had matters of his own to attend to—not least the fact that as he'd essentially condemned his day tomorrow he had work to do tonight.

He strode back to the Range Rover, dropped the box of cigars into the glove box, and then hesitated before sliding behind the wheel. If Francesca was on her way back to the Abbey, she must be using the old bridle-way, he reflected. Otherwise he would have seen her on the road.

He scowled.

Why was he hesitating? It was still light, and the bridle-way was a perfectly safe means of walking between the Abbey and the village. Good heavens, in the early years after Francesca had first come to live at Lingard, they had often gone walking there themselves, with the dogs. In fact, the paths around here were a regular haunt for lovers.

And peeping Toms!

His jaw compressed and, slamming the car door, he strode across the green to St Mary's churchyard. A pair of metal posts to one side of the churchyard signalled the entrance to the bridle-way. The posts had been put there by the parish council to prevent any means of transport other than horses and cycles from gaining access to the footpath, and he passed between them with scarcely a thought for his vehicle, which was still illegally parked on the green. His mind was focused on one thing and one thing only, and although he kept telling himself that this was just another example of Francesca's thoughtlessness anxiety had a stranglehold on his nerves.

Beyond the wall of the churchyard, the bridle-way plunged into a copse of willows and aspens that skirted the banks of the river, and Will's stomach tightened at the realisation that he hadn't given the river a thought. But why should he? he argued with himself impatiently. It wasn't as if Francesca had left the Abbey in a great state of distress. When he and Emma had encountered her on the stairs, she had seemed uncommonly composed to him. Certainly, she hadn't had to think twice about explaining her appearance, whereas he had been momentarily lost for words.

He paused for a moment, scanning the riverbank, but apart from a pair of grey squirrels and a family of ducks there didn't seem to be any sign of life. Perhaps she was just wasting his time, he thought irritably. He wasn't going to find her. Not until she chose to show herself, that was.

With a muttered exclamation he started back towards the churchyard, and that was when he saw the ripple of bronze silk. He almost missed it, partially hidden as it was among the reeds and grasses that grew half in, half out of the water. But he recognised it at once as the shirt Francesca had been wearing earlier in the day. It was like a blow to his solar plexus, and without a moment's hesitation he plunged down the slope to where the garment was lying.

But it wasn't just a garment he had seen, he realised

almost instantly. The angle of the bank, and the screen of vegetation, had deceived him into thinking the shirt had been discarded; but it hadn't. As he got nearer, he could see that it was Francesca herself who was lying on the bank, and for a moment he had the awful fear that she was dead.

'God—'

The word burst from his lips as he reached her, and in those first few seconds time seemed to stand still. She looked so pale, her lashes dark fans against her creamy white cheeks, it didn't seem possible that she was still breathing, and he fell onto his knees beside her, his hand reaching out automatically to cup her cheek.

She started violently, and he jerked back onto his haunches, almost as shocked as she obviously was at being disturbed. 'Will,' she said finally, her tongue appearing to moisten her lips in apparent confusion. 'Oh, God! You scared me.'

Will breathed deeply. 'You scared me,' he countered, trying to control a sudden surge of anger at this evidence of her irresponsibility. He swallowed the bile that had risen into his throat. 'What the—what—exactly—do you think you're doing?'

CHAPTER SEVEN

WILL was mad—and with good reason, thought Francesca ruefully. As she struggled into a sitting position, she took a swift glance at her watch and saw it was already after six o'clock. How could she have forgotten the time in such circumstances? She must have nodded off for a few minutes. Would he accept exhaustion as a convincing excuse?

'I've hurt my ankle,' she muttered, realising how weak it sounded. Particularly as the swelling had to some extent subsided, and she might have been able to walk on it if she'd taken care.

Will stared at her without sympathy. 'You've hurt your ankle?' he echoed, without much conviction, although his dark gaze did seek out the shoe she had discarded earlier. 'How the hell did you hurt your ankle? Did you slip?'

'The undergrowth is damp,' she said at last, unwilling to admit that she had been foolish enough to try to reach the water. But it had looked so cool and inviting, and she hadn't thought about the dangers when she'd started down the bank.

'So you did slip!' he exclaimed disgustedly. 'And, I suppose, you twisted your ankle in the process.'

'Something like that.' Francesca was defensive, and Will shook his head in disbelief.

'And I suppose you've been sitting there waiting for me to come and find you.' He blew out a breath. 'My God, and I was worried about you. I should have had more sense.'

'What do you mean?'

'What do I mean?' He pressed his palms down on his

78

spread thighs and got abruptly to his feet. 'Why didn't you walk back to the village as that was nearer? Why didn't you call the Abbey, or if not that a cab?'

Francesca gave an indignant snort as she looked up at him. 'Why d'you think?' she demanded, massaging her aching foot. 'Will, whether you believe it or not, I did try to get back up the bank again, but I couldn't. I thought if I sat here for a while it might stop hurting so much.'

'Ah.' He was sardonic. 'And it never crossed your mind that people might be concerned? Or were you hoping to cause a scandal? LOCAL LORD'S EX-WIFE FOUND PROSTRATE ON RIVERBANK perhaps?'

'You're a sarcastic devil,' said Francesca resentfully. 'I wasn't exactly happy about being stuck here myself. And I'd have thought twice about ringing the Abbey anyway. I wouldn't have wanted to interrupt your afternoon.'

Will pushed his hands into his jacket pockets. 'But you're all right now, I assume.'

'Why would you assume that?'

'Well, for someone who was uneasy, you weren't exactly safety-conscious, were you?' he retorted shortly. 'For God's sake, Fran, didn't it occur to you that you might not be as safe here as you think? What if this man, whoever he is, had found you? You were *asleep* when I first saw you. Goddammit, anything could have happened to you.'

Francesca's face mirrored her distress and, glimpsing a certain remorse in his expression, she guessed he was regretting being quite so outspoken in his criticism. 'Y-you don't think *he* could have followed me here, do you?' she exclaimed, everything else forgotten in the horror of that thought. She got painfully to her feet, wincing as she was forced to put her weight on the injured ankle. 'Dear God, I never thought of that.'

Will made an impatient gesture. 'No,' he said, with some asperity. 'No, I don't think he has a cat in hell's chance of finding you here. But he's not the only pervert in the country.' He looked at her half contemptuously. 'Is this a silly question, or can you walk?'

Francesca held up her head. 'I can try.' She took a tentative step, and turned her face away so he wouldn't see the involuntary grimace she made. 'Slowly,' she added, after a moment, giving herself time to recover. 'But I don't think I can make it to the house.'

'No one's asking you to,' declared Will, regarding her with some misgivings. 'Here—' He moved towards her. 'Take my arm. The Rover's only about a couple of hundred yards away.'

Only!

Francesca gritted her teeth and forced a tight smile. 'That's good,' she said, having to take his arm in spite of her reluctance to touch him. 'Just don't expect me to go at your pace.'

Will gave her another doubtful look, and then turned to her with frustration in his eyes. 'Okay,' he said, removing her hand from his arm, 'I'll carry you. I just hope the old lady doesn't get to hear about this.'

'There's no need for—'

But before she could finish what she had been about to say Will had deftly swung her off her feet. She was obviously lighter than she thought, or maybe he was stronger than she remembered, she reflected ruefully. Whatever, it was a relief not to have to put her weight on her foot again.

All the same, there were definite disadvantages to being carried by a man whom she had once sworn never to speak to again. All right, so he had been the first person she had thought of turning to in the present situation, but, she reminded herself, that was as much because of distance as anything else. And, yes, she'd known that she could trust him. In this, at least, she amended reluctantly. Five years ago, she might have viewed things differently.

Now, however, she had been put in the ignominious

position of having to depend on him totally, and, no
matter that she might have preferred not to get this close
to him, she didn't have much choice but to hang on. As
he climbed up onto the path again, it would have been
difficult not to wrap her arms around his neck for safety.
God knew, she didn't want him to drop her, and it was
a precarious climb.

He was breathing quite heavily when they reached the
path, the masculine heat of his body unwillingly familiar
to her. He still used the same deodorant, she noticed, its
odour mingling with the clean sweat he was exuding,
which was causing the back of his neck to become quite
damp.

As soon as they reached the path, Francesca removed
her hands from his neck, but not without becoming
aware that his scent was now on her fingers, too. The
realisation aroused two quite different impulses: the first
was to scrub her fingers against his collar and remove
any trace of moisture from them, and the second was to
bring her fingers to her lips and sample his individual
taste.

She did neither, of course, although when Will turned
his head to ask if she was all right the warmth of his
breath was unbearably sweet. Dear God, she thought, did
he have any idea how much he still disturbed her? Had
he any notion of how tempting it was to anticipate how
he would react if she tried to turn his kindness to her
advantage?

But to what advantage? she asked herself impatiently
as he strode past St Mary's churchyard. What advantage
was there in trying to make Will desire her again? Did
she really want him to know she had such thoughts about
him—still? Wasn't it more sensible to leave well alone?

Of course it was, and common sense quickly disposed
of any lingering regret at what might have been. Her
visit here was not at his invitation; she had to remember
that. Whatever had gone before, he didn't deserve that
she should repay his charity by disrupting his life.

'Have your guests gone?' she asked, deciding that was a fairly innocuous question, and he gave her a narrow-eyed stare.

'Yes,' he replied. 'They left about an hour ago. They're staying at Mulberry Court, as a matter of fact.'

'Now why doesn't that surprise me?' remarked Francesca drily, unable to keep the sarcasm out of her tone. She bit her lip in annoyance, and started again. 'Who are they? I thought the younger woman was very pretty.'

'Don't be so patronising,' said Will curtly, and she guessed she had scraped a nerve. 'I don't see that it matters to you who they are, but if you must know their name is Merritt.' He paused at the end of the bridle-way. 'I'm going to put you down now.'

'Because I asked who your guests were?' she queried indignantly, and Will gave her a repressive look.

'Because I'm going to turn the Rover round and pick you up,' he retorted, depositing her beside one of the iron posts. 'Wait here. I won't be a minute.'

Francesca spent the few moments it took him to turn the vehicle wondering how she was going to climb up into the car. But, in the event, she didn't have to. Will left the engine running, swung open his door, and came and lifted her into the passenger seat.

As he drove back to the Abbey, Francesca couldn't help speculating over what he had told her. If all three of his guests had been called Merritt, then it seemed fairly obvious that they were from the same family. Which meant—what? She cast him a sideways glance. That Lady Rosemary was matchmaking? Was the fact that the Merritts were staying with his grandmother just a coincidence? Or had Will himself arranged it after meeting the younger woman somewhere else?

The idea wasn't appealing. The trouble was, the longer she stayed here, the harder it was for her to regard Will with the objectivity she had cultivated over the past five years. Familiarity might breed contempt, but it also bred informality. She was rapidly beginning to resent her own sequestration. Dear God, she thought irritably, pretty soon she'd forget why she'd come here at all.

As if sensing her unease, Will glanced her way at that moment, his lean, intelligent features registering a certain caution at the sight of her expression. 'What?' he asked, arching a dark brow. 'I get the feeling you want to say something. If it's about Emma, you can forget it. She doesn't know who you are.'

Francesca caught her breath. 'As if I'd think she did,' she declared tartly, totally forgetting her intention to be impartial. 'I knew you wouldn't tell her who I was.'

Will blew out a breath. 'Oh?' he said evenly. 'Why?'

Francesca cast him a defensive look. 'Because I imagine you and she are—well, intimate. And I doubt if your girlfriend would appreciate knowing your ex-wife is staying at your house.'

Will took a deep breath. 'We're not sleeping together, if that's what you're insinuating,' he told her shortly. 'And she's not my girlfriend. I hardly know the woman. I've only met her twice.'

'Really?' Francesca crushed the feeling of relief his words had given her beneath an unforgivable display of irony. 'Well, don't look now, darling, but I'm sure she knows exactly what you are!'

Will's eyes darkened for a moment, and then a trace of humour touched his mouth. 'Jealous?' he enquired, watching her reaction.

And, deciding to be honest, Francesca murmured, 'Maybe.'

His disbelief was palpable, and Francesca was belatedly glad of it. She didn't know what had possessed her to admit such a thing, or what she might have said if Will had taken her up on her remark. In any case, their arrival back at the Abbey curtailed any further developments, and she told herself she was glad not to have to explain.

She had slid down from the vehicle before he had time

to cut the engine and come round to help her, and she was hobbling across to the entrance when he reached her.

'Do you need any help?' he asked, but she just favoured him with a shake of her head before disappearing from his sight into the house.

An hour and a luxurious soak in the bath later Francesca was feeling considerably better, physically, at least. Certainly better than she'd felt the previous day at this time, she acknowledged gratefully, wrapping a soft white towel around her and walking painfully into the bedroom. Even the lingering discomfort in her ankle was preferable to the emotional trauma she had experienced the night before, and she wondered if she hadn't been the slightest bit hysterical when she'd found that broken window.

After all, as Clare's husband had pointed out, she didn't actually know it was the stalker who had attempted to break into the flat. It could have been vandals, he'd insisted. Living alone, going out to work every day, she was likely to be a target. She should wait until she'd calmed down before doing anything rash.

But Francesca hadn't listened to him. He and Clare didn't know about the phone call, so they couldn't understand why she'd wanted to get away. Perhaps she'd been wrong; perhaps she had been over-sensitive. In retrospect it was much easier to take a rational view.

All the same, it wasn't a vandal who had been terrorising her. It wasn't a vandal who had made all those ugly phone calls, describing in great detail what he was going to do with her when he was good and ready. Her skin crawled at the memory of the sordid things he had said to her, and for all her brave attempt at confidence she could feel her efforts slipping away.

Unable to contemplate the future with any degree of optimism, Francesca slumped down onto the dressing table stool and regarded her reflection in the mirror.

Then, picking up her brush, she dragged it through her loosened hair. Dammit, she thought, she had to get a hold of herself. Giving in to his harassment was only playing into his hands.

With thoughts like these preying on her mind, she decided there was no way she could eat in her room this evening. Whether Will liked it or not, she needed to talk to someone—*anyone*. She'd rather eat in the kitchen with Mrs Harvey than up here on her own.

Which meant she was forced to put on the suit she had been wearing when she'd arrived. Although she had got one or two personal items in the village, she had had no luck as far as supplementing her wardrobe was concerned. She regretted not having brought a dress or another skirt with her, and then chided herself for caring what she looked like in the present situation.

Heels were out of the question, however, and when she descended the stairs a few minutes later she was self-consciously aware of how incongruous her Doc Martens looked with her suit. Still, she consoled herself, at least they were reasonably comfortable, and no one could accuse her of putting vanity before good sense.

The hall was empty, as was the drawing room when she chanced a look inside. It was possible that Will was eating out again this evening, but surely if he had been he'd have said as much to her.

Yet why should he? She had come here uninvited and unannounced, and he had every right to get on with his life as if she didn't exist. She knew, from her own experience, that he was not short of friends, and as the local squire he was expected to attend all manner of social events.

She bit her lip and hobbled back across the hall to the library. The door was closed and, dismissing the urge to tap politely for admittance, she turned the handle and pushed the heavy door open. To her relief—or to her chagrin; it depended which way you looked at it, she decided ruefully—Will was sprawled behind his desk taking a phone call. He hadn't changed his clothes since that afternoon, and his brows arched almost mockingly when he saw her.

She would have withdrawn again, but he lifted an imperious hand and waved her into the room. 'This won't take long,' he said, putting his hand across the mouthpiece and waving her to a seat. 'Help yourself to a drink,' he added, and she noticed the quarter-full whisky tumbler that was standing on the desk in front of him.

Although she wasn't keen on whisky in the normal way, tonight a stiffener seemed in order. Adding an equal measure of ice and water to her glass, she took a tentative taste, grimacing as the spirit caught the back of her throat.

By the time she had seated herself in one of the leather armchairs that flanked the fireplace, Will had finished his call. Swallowing the remainder of the whisky in his glass, he went to pour himself another, before coming to stand on the hearth nearby.

'How's the ankle?' he asked, and Francesca found herself colouring a little as he took in the clunky shoes.

'Much better,' she said. 'I took a bath, and I think the warmth has reduced the swelling. In any case, I can walk on it again, and that's the main thing.'

'Hmm.'

Will regarded her for a few more moments, and she wondered what he was thinking. That she should have warned him if she was coming down for supper, perhaps? Or was he thinking of her foolish response to his enquiry if she was jealous?

'I hope it's not a problem if I have my meal downstairs this evening?' she ventured at last, aware that the silence between them wasn't getting any easier. 'I can eat in the kitchen, if Mrs Harvey doesn't mind. I realise you're probably going out.'

'I'm not going out,' replied Will flatly. 'And even if I were you can't seriously expect me to believe that you think I'd ask you to do something like that.' He gave her an impatient look. 'Your arrival may have been un-expected, but you're still my guest and, as such, you'll be treated with as much respect as anyone else.'

'Well, thanks.' Francesca pulled a wry face. 'But if you had been going out I'd have preferred Watkins' or Mrs Harvey's company to my own, if you see what I mean.'

'Ah.' Will's dark brows descended. 'You're still upset about what happened yesterday?'

'Something like that.' Francesca took another gulp of her whisky and found it rather more palatable this time. 'In any case, I'd rather not talk about it. I'm sure you must be as sick as I am of the whole affair.'

'I wouldn't say that.' Will moved away to stand at the window, and she felt a small sense of relief. 'At least it makes a change from my problems,' he added drily. 'But go on; tell me about what you've been doing these last five years instead.'

'Oh—' Francesca was surprised at his question. 'Well, you know what I've been doing—more or less. After doing some temporary work, I got a job with Teniko, and I've been with them for about four years.'

Will turned to rest his shoulder against the frame. 'You live alone, I gather.'

'Yes.' Francesca told herself she had no right to feel resentful of his enquiry. 'I live in a one-bedroomed flat in Kensington, which I've never shared with anyone else. Except Jamaica.'

'Jamaica?'

Will's eyes had narrowed, and she sighed. 'My cat,' she said, despising the image it initiated. 'He was knocked down and killed three months ago, and I haven't had the heart to replace him.'

'Killed?' Will frowned. 'Who killed him?'

'Who?' She looked puzzled. 'I don't know. They didn't stop. I just found him lying at the side of the road when I got home from work.' Her throat tightened. 'That wasn't a good day either.'

Will nodded. 'I see.'

But something in his tone disturbed her. 'You don't
think— Oh, no!' Her throat closed up entirely. 'You
don't think someone did it on purpose?'

Will looked as if he regretted making the connection
now. 'Probably not,' he said as she took refuge in her
glass. 'Here…' He came towards her, holding out his
hand. 'Let me get you another. We've got at least another half-hour before supper is ready.'

She let him refill her glass, primarily to give herself
time to assimilate what he had said. She had been stupid,
perhaps, but it had never occurred to her that Jamaica's
death might not have been the unfortunate accident she'd
believed it to be. Yet, now she came to think of it, it
was just after that that she had started getting the threatening calls.

Will brought her glass back to her, and she took it
from him delicately, avoiding his hands. Then he seated
himself in the chair opposite, legs splayed, his glass cradled between his palms. He regarded her thoughtfully,
evidently aware that his words had disturbed her, and
eager to make amends. She wished she could just close
her eyes and make it all go away, not least Will himself,
and the treacherous emotions he still aroused in her.

'So,' he said, with studied nonchalance, 'you're not
thinking of getting married again?'

Francesca schooled her features. She hadn't realised
how hard it would be to conduct a casual conversation
with Will, and she was beginning to wonder if she had
been entirely wise in coming downstairs. They knew one
another too well, and it was difficult to hide things from
him. Yet she couldn't pretend they were friends—not
after what had gone before.

One of his shirt buttons had become unfastened, she
noticed, exposing an errant tuft of dark hair. Through
the fine material of his shirt, she could see the shadow
of the hair that arrowed down to his navel, sense the
muscled body that she had once known as intimately as

her own. She might not want to notice such things, but she couldn't seem to help it, no more than she could ignore the impressive mound between his legs.

'I'm not thinking of getting married again, no,' she said at last, hurrying into speech in an effort to distract her wayward thoughts. 'But you are,' she added recklessly. 'That was—Miss Merritt you were speaking to on the phone, wasn't it?'

CHAPTER EIGHT

WILL'S eyes cooled considerably. 'As a matter of fact, it was my grandmother,' he corrected her shortly. 'She'd heard—don't ask me how—that you were missing. She wanted to know if you'd left for good.'

Francesca's mouth drew in. 'And you had to disappoint her,' she said, with assumed bravado, and Will wished he didn't feel so damned defensive on her behalf. He'd just spent the last fifteen minutes justifying his concern to his grandmother, and he resented her implication that he shared Lady Rosemary's opinion.

Even if he should.

'Who knows what does or doesn't disappoint the old lady?' he replied after a moment, unwilling to get into that kind of argument with her. 'Suffice it to say that I've always disappointed her in one way or the other. You'd think she'd have realised I'm a lost cause by now, but she just keeps plugging away.'

Francesca's expression softened. 'No one could call you a lost cause, Will,' she said, her hand continually smoothing the leather arm of the chair an indication of her nervous state. She forced a smile. 'You're her blue-eyed boy—metaphorically, of course. I'm surprised she hasn't achieved her objective already. I can't believe Miss Merritt is the first candidate she's produced.'

Will's lips thinned. 'You may not realise it, but you're a lot like my grandmother yourself,' he declared tersely. 'Once you get your teeth into something, you insist on worrying it to death. And for God's sake, stop calling Emma Miss Merritt. I don't remember you being so formal before.'

'That's because we were never in this situation be-

90

fore,' she informed him stiffly, her hair catching the light as she tilted her head. Once again, it was drawn back from her face, but she'd left two silky strands to fall at either side of her temple, and he pondered its unusual colouring that was neither red nor gold. 'When we were at college, it was different,' she continued. 'You were just Will Quentin then. You behaved like all the other students. I didn't know you owned this place, or that you had an ancient title to uphold.'

Will lay back in his chair, propping one ankle on his knee and regarding her with narrowed eyes. 'We worked it out,' he remarked mildly. 'Come on, Fran. Stop making excuses. We know one another far too well to stand on ceremony now.'

'Your grandmother doesn't think so.'

Will made an impatient sound. 'How do you know what my grandmother thinks?' he demanded, even though it was true. 'And why does it matter to you what the old lady thinks? What does she have to do with us? What did she ever have to do with us?'

'She hates me,' said Francesca simply, and Will's foot dropped to the floor in arrant disbelief.

'Now I know you're being foolish,' he said impatiently. He swung forward in his chair. 'Okay. I know you and the old lady never saw eye to eye about things, but believing that she hates you is crazy.'

Francesca sipped her whisky. 'If you say so.' But she didn't sound convinced.

'I do say so.' Will felt a trace of aggravation. 'I have it on good authority that she's concerned about you. She wants this matter clearing up as much as you do.'

'But for different reasons,' persisted Francesca, looking at him over the rim of her glass. 'Oh, all right, Will, I don't want to talk about your grandmother any more than you do. What she thinks doesn't matter any more. You started this conversation, not me.'

'I'd dispute that,' said Will irritably, and then once again her haunted expression made him draw back.

Dammit, she had enough on her plate without him un-
loading some of his own frustration. Why couldn't they
have a normal conversation instead of dragging up all
the debris of the past?

'So,' she said, after a moment, circling the rim of her
glass with a delicate finger, 'are you going to marry
Miss—Emma?'

Will blew out a breath, aware that he was more disturbed by that circling finger than by anything she'd
said. She had long, slender fingers, and, dammit, he
could still remember how those fingers had looked
against his skin. How they'd felt, too, he acknowledged,
feeling his body hardening. Oh, God, he thought disgustedly, didn't he have any more control over himself
than this?

Francesca had looked up now, and, aware that he
couldn't allow her to see what was happening to him,
he got abruptly to his feet. Turning his back on her, he
walked over to his previous position by the windows,
and then, realising she was still waiting for a reply, he
said guardedly, 'Does it matter?'

'No.' Her response was unflatteringly dismissive. 'I
was just trying to make conversation, that's all. But you
have to admit it's something you've been thinking about.
Unless you make a habit of entertaining young women
and their parents.'

Will sighed, and, having succeeded in getting control
of himself again, he turned to face her. 'My grandmother
would like a great-grandchild,' he conceded flatly. 'You
were not prepared to appease her, so I must.'

Francesca suddenly went very pale. 'You couldn't
wait to bring that up, could you?' she asked, her lips
tight and colourless. 'Just when I thought we were having a polite conversation, you had to make that nasty
little comment and spoil everything.' She thrust her glass
aside, spilling a little of the whisky in the process, and
then pushed herself to her feet and started painfully for
the door. 'I've decided I will eat upstairs, if it's all the

same to you. My own company's not as unpleasant as yours.'

'Fran—'

He caught hold of her arm before she could reach for the handle, and although she probably would have liked to wrench herself away from him she considered her ankle and remained where she was. But she was as stiff as a board, her whole body a tightly strung ball of resistance, and Will wondered how their civil exchange had come to this.

'I'm sorry,' he said, uneasily aware of how fragile her arm seemed within the sleeve of her jacket. He had the feeling that if he exerted too much pressure the arm might break. In her shirt and jeans, which were probably too big for her anyway, she had appeared rather more sturdy. Though he remembered that when he'd lifted her she'd felt no weight at all.

'It doesn't matter.'

But it did, and he knew it. 'Come and sit down again?' he said persuasively, trying to lighten the situation. 'You're right. I'm a tactless oaf. You've got enough to contend with as it is.'

'It's not your concern,' she said tightly, clearly not prepared to accept his apology. 'Will you speak to Mrs Harvey or shall I?'

A graphic swear word slid unrestrainedly from his lips, and without thinking too intelligently about what he was about to do Will drew her round to face him. Then, pulling her towards him, he wrapped his arms about her, pressing her head into his shoulder, his hand stroking the back of her neck.

She didn't struggle, but then neither did she respond in any way. She let him take her and hold her, but she made no attempt to reciprocate. Her hands hung loosely by her sides, and her spine was rigid. It was like holding a flesh-and-blood statue, and Will gave an inward groan at the damage he had caused.

'Fran,' he said again, his fingers at her nape brushing

the silky knot of hair, and finding the erratic pulse that belied her unyielding form. 'God, Fran, you know I wouldn't hurt you. But it's not easy coming to terms with the fact that you're actually here.'

'I didn't ask you to let me stay,' she mumbled against his throat, her lips moistening the fine silk of his shirt, and his body clenched.

'I know that,' he muttered, wishing he weren't so conscious of her nearness. But the touch of her skirt against his legs was absurdly familiar, and when he bent his head towards her her delicate scent rose sweetly into his nostrils. His lips grazed her soft cheek, and he tasted the salt of tears on her skin. 'Oh, Fran,' he groaned, 'stop fighting me, will you? At least let me give you some comfort, if nothing else.'

'I don't want your comfort,' she said through clenched teeth, turning her face away from him, as if she was afraid he was going to kiss her. *Kiss her?* His stomach tightened. He badly wanted to shake her—and then pull her down onto the sofa and make mad, passionate love to her, he finished with bitter candour.

'You don't know what you want,' he told her now, the harshness in his voice an indication of the strain he was feeling. But, dammit, he was letting her weakness and her frailty undermine his sanity, and it briefly crossed his mind that if Lady Rosemary could see him now she'd very likely have a seizure. 'This business with this man has made you hypersensitive to any criticism,' he continued firmly. 'I'm a clumsy fool, I know that, but don't let it—spoil things between us.'

'Spoil things between *us?*' She repeated his words in a strangled voice, and suddenly her hands came up to press against his chest. 'Between us, Will?' she said again, staring at him with tear-washed eyes. 'Haven't you forgotten something? There is no *us!* Just you—and me—and a whole history of lies and deceit!'

Will's fingers gripped her shoulders. 'It wasn't like that,' he said roughly, aware that he was taking this further—much further—than he had intended. But she was so damned appealing in her distress, her eyes wide, her lashes spiky with unshed tears, her mouth soft and moist, a bewitching temptation in itself.

Before he knew what he was doing, he had leant towards her and brushed her mouth with his. Once, twice, he rubbed his lips over hers, before covering her mouth completely and slipping his tongue between her teeth.

His senses swam; heat, hot and sensual, rose to cloud his brain. He was not thinking clearly, he would tell himself afterwards, or he wouldn't have done it, but whatever madness had gripped him was too strong for him to resist.

For her part, she had obviously not been expecting him to kiss her, and for a moment she did nothing but stand impassively beneath his sensuous assault. It was as if the unexpected pressure of his mouth on hers had nullified whatever protest she might have made, and that there was some latent need still inside her that made her briefly forget how she'd come to be in this position.

Whatever, as he continued to hold her, he felt her resistance weakening. Her mouth softened, became responsive, sought mindlessly for its own reward. Her hands spread against his chest, and, finding an opening in his shirt, her nails scraped painfully over his hot skin. But he never felt the scratch, only the sensual pleasure it gave him, and he felt her heartbeat accelerating as his hands slid down her back.

The memories were instantaneous. They fitted together so perfectly. They always had. Time had no meaning as his hands found the hem of her skirt and slid beneath it, finding the taut curve of her bottom, and bringing her fully against him for the first time. His fingertips snagged the hem of her panties, and he remembered how she had always preferred stockings to tights. Silk, fine and lace-trimmed, they invited his slightly unsteady invasion, and he allowed the pad of his thumb to find the delicious cleft between her legs.

She was wet.

His breathing constricted as the scent of her rose sweetly to his nostrils, hot and musky, and wildly desirable. A groan welled in his throat. He wanted her then, wanted her so badly it hurt. His body ached for hers in a way it had never ached for anyone else. He remembered so well how good it had been to feel her tight muscles opening for him, enfolding him, rippling voluptuously when she came. Her climax had driven him to the very edge of insanity before his own blissful release had had him convulsing in her arms, and however crazy this was he needed to feel that release again.

His blood beat thickly in his head, the yielding softness of her slim body deafening him to the clamour of his rational senses. He didn't care about anything at that moment; didn't care what happened in the future, so long as his immediate needs were satisfied.

But then, as if the sudden heavy heat of his arousal against her stomach brought its own awareness, she uttered a muffled moan and jack-knifed away from him. Wrapping her arms around herself, as if she was afraid she was about to fall apart, she shook her head almost disbelievingly. 'Why?' she demanded, in a hoarse voice. 'Why did you do that?'

Because I couldn't stop myself. Because I still want you. Because all I can think about is how hot and tight you were, and how much I want to bury myself between your sweet thighs...

'Why d'you think?' he said instead, dragging himself back from the unguarded precipice of his own weakness. As she stared at him, her contempt clear in her eyes, he was appalled at what had so nearly happened. For God's sake, he chided himself bitterly, was he going to let a purely physical need destroy the very real peace of mind he'd found in recent months? He wanted her, yes, but not, he told himself savagely, *not* that much.

'I don't know, do I?' she retorted, obviously not prepared to let him off the hook. 'How—how could you?'

Will drew a hoarse breath. 'Why not?' He managed an indifferent shrug of his shoulders. 'I'm sorry. I thought you needed—reassurance.'

'Reassurance?' She spoke faintly. '*That* was reassurance?'

'That you're still an attractive woman,' he agreed, feeling in desperate need of another drink. 'Don't look at me like that, Fran. It was no big deal. We've been married, remember? I kissed you, that's all. Don't make it more—important than it was.'

She made a strangled sound. 'Will, you had your tongue in my mouth!' She paused. 'You—you touched me.'

'So?' He was defensive now. 'I'm not denying it.' He raked back his hair with a nervous hand. 'Don't tell me you haven't wondered how it would feel if we—if we were close again.'

She swallowed. 'Do you mean—intimate?'

'I mean close,' he said tightly, his throat closing up with the images she was evoking. 'Fran—'

'You mean you have?' she asked incredulously, and he stifled a groan.

'All right. Sure.'

'You have?'

'Of course.' He tried to sound casual.

'Why?'

'Why?' God, he needed that drink. 'Why not? We were together for a long time, Fran. It's only natural that seeing you again should arouse old—old—'

'Feelings?'

'Memories,' he said flatly. 'Look, can I get you another drink? I think we could both use one.'

'Not for me,' she was saying stiffly when there was a knock at the door.

What timing, Will thought drily, going to open it himself. The last thing he wanted was for Watkins or Mrs Harvey to come in here and see that Francesca had been crying. Hell, he could imagine what an interesting piece of gossip that would be to pass on to Mulberry Court.

As he'd expected, it was Watkins, and the old man looked a little taken aback when his employer confronted him. 'Excuse me, my lord!' he exclaimed in surprise, and Will was well aware that the old butler was trying his best to look over his shoulder and into the room behind him. 'Um—I just came to tell you that—er—supper's ready when you are, my lord.'

'Thank you.' Will managed a polite smile. 'We'll be along in a few minutes.'

'Er—Mrs Quentin is with you, my lord?'

'She is.' Will started to close the door. 'Is that all?'

Watkins stuttered, 'Um—I—er—yes, my lord.'

'Good.'

Realising he was acting out of character, Will closed the door in the old man's face, and then rested back against it for a moment before starting out across the room to the drinks tray. Pouring himself another stiff drink, he swallowed half of it at a gulp, and then, propping his hip against the table, he stared unseeingly out of the window. He had really done it now, he thought, contempt for himself flooding his senses. Whatever had possessed him to do it? To grab her, and kiss her, as if he was starved for the sight and feel of her, to drop his guard so completely that he was in very real danger of losing what little credibility he had left?

'You don't honestly expect me to have supper with you?'

Francesca's husky protest came to him as if from a great distance, and it took a supreme effort of will to turn and face her with any degree of equanimity. 'Why not?' he enquired, managing to keep all expression out of his voice. His dark brows ascended with deliberate irony. 'You're not afraid of me, are you?'

'Afraid of you?' That had her briefly speechless. 'No. No, I'm not afraid of you.'

'Well, then?'

'Will, please stop pretending that nothing's happened here.' A pink tongue appeared to wet lips that were already as moist as a ripe peach. 'Never mind supper; I think I ought to leave.'

His stomach contracted. 'And go back to London?'

'Where else?' But he could tell the prospect was not as attractive to her as she might pretend. 'If I leave now, I can be in London by eleven—'

'No!' Will's brain sought urgently for some excuse to justify his denial. 'That would be foolish, wouldn't it? I mean—' he thought rapidly '—do you really want to return to your flat at night, in the dark, not knowing what you're going to find?'

'You mean *him*, don't you?' Francesca stared at him with wounded eyes. 'That's an awful thing to suggest, Will.'

It was, and he knew it, but desperate needs demanded desperate measures. 'Well—what about your ankle?' he exclaimed with sudden inspiration, wishing he had thought of it first. 'You can't drive all that way with only one foot.'

Francesca frowned, but she cast a doubtful glance at her ankle. Although she obviously would have liked to contradict him, the truth was the ankle was still swollen—more now, since she had been standing on it, than before.

'I'm not an invalid,' she said tersely, but she was clearly hesitating, and Will pushed his advantage.

'Look,' he said, shoving his hands into his jacket pockets, 'you have every right to feel angry about what happened, and I'm sorry. I don't know what came over me. I felt sorry for you, I guess, and I just wanted you to know that—that, well, I'm here for you, I suppose.'

Francesca's lips twisted. 'Here for me?' she echoed sarcastically. Her eyes dropped to his crotch. 'As in if I want sex, do you mean?'

'No.' His jaw compressed. 'Dammit, Fran, I'm only human. What do you expect of me? Divine abstinence?'

Francesca pressed her lips together. 'No,' she said carefully. 'Just—just friendship, that's all. Is that so much to ask?'

CHAPTER NINE

FRANCESCA slept badly.

Despite the fact that she and Will had managed to achieve a kind of armed truce for the remainder of the evening, when she eventually crawled into bed she found it almost impossible to relax. And for the first time in months it was not fear of the stalker that disrupted her rest. It was the thought of what had happened between her and Will in the library, and the uneasy suspicion that even after all that had happened she was still pathetically vulnerable where he was concerned.

Of course she denied it, and she spent a considerable length of time berating herself for being such a fool. She was vulnerable at the moment, but not because of anything Will had done. In her circumstances, anyone would be vulnerable, and it was only natural that she should feel—gratitude towards Will because he'd helped her.

The truth was—he'd said it—he felt sorry for her. He was a decent man, and no decent man would wish her situation on his worst enemy. She had been his wife for almost five years, and they had lived together before that, so naturally he felt some sense of pity for her. However acrimonious their parting had ultimately been, he couldn't completely erase the past.

And he hadn't intended to kiss her. She knew that. He'd intended to comfort her, that was all, and things had got a little out of hand. They knew one another too well, she thought: that was the trouble. When he'd covered her lips with his, she'd wanted desperately to respond.

Which was why she awakened the next morning with an acutely hung-over feeling, a sense of something ominous hanging over her head. The prospect of seeing Will again was not appealing. She'd have much preferred to bury her head under the pillows and stay where she was.

Of course she awakened most mornings aware of a sense of dread, these days, but this was different. For once, thoughts of the man who had been harassing her were not in the forefront of her mind. She had the feeling that whatever had happened the night before it had irrevocably altered their situation. That, no matter what she did, things would never be quite the same again.

She made an impatient sound, pushing herself up on her elbows and looking around the room. As usual, she was overreacting, she thought disgustedly. She doubted if Will was subjecting himself to this kind of soul-searching, just because he'd made a pass at his ex-wife. She ought to get things in perspective. She was only thinking about it now because she didn't want to think about having to leave.

To leave...

Her stomach hollowed abruptly. That was true enough: she didn't want to leave, and the real horror of the situation was that she had to go back. Back to London, back to her flat, back to those awful phone calls. Oh, God, she thought sickly, what was she going to do?

She swung her legs out of bed, unable to relax any longer. But when she attempted to get to her feet she let out an involuntary moan. She'd forgotten about her injured ankle, but it was obvious it was still not completely cured.

'Damn...' she muttered, and then started as usual when there was a tentative tap at her door. She guessed it was probably Mrs Harvey, but she still perched on the side of the bed and wrapped the quilt protectively about her. Old habits die hard, she thought uneasily, and her nerves were strung as taut as violin strings.

The door opened without warning, however, and the housekeeper stuck her head round, as if expecting Francesca to be asleep. 'Oh, you're awake, madam!' she exclaimed, not without a trace of embarrassment. 'I was just checking. I came up earlier but you were dead to the world.'

An unfortunate choice of words, reflected Francesca ruefully, but she didn't comment on it. Instead, she looked at the clock, her eyes widening in amazement when she saw the time.

'Good Lord,' she said, half disbelievingly. 'It's half past nine!'

'Like I said,' agreed Mrs Harvey, pushing the door wider and folding her arms across her ample bosom, 'I came up earlier, with your tea, but you were sound asleep.'

'Oh, I'm sorry.' Francesca felt awful now. 'I hope I haven't put you to any trouble. It took me some time last night to get to sleep.'

'Of course it hasn't put me to any trouble,' declared the housekeeper firmly. 'You needed the rest, and it's not as if there's anything spoiling. His lordship himself said not to wake you. He said to tell you he'd be back about five, and if there's anything you need in the meantime either Edna or myself will see to it for you.'

Francesca swallowed. 'W—he's gone out?'

'His lordship? Yes, madam. I believe he's taking Miss Merritt to York for the day. In any event, he said that you should take things easy.' She smiled. 'He's most concerned about you, madam. But I expect you know that.'

Did she?

Francesca pressed her lips together. What was she to think when he knew she'd planned to drive back to London today, leaving a day earlier than they'd originally agreed? Yet wasn't it typical of Will to present her with a *fait accompli*? If she left now, she wouldn't see him again.

'Anyway, I'll go and get your tray now,' said Mrs Harvey, evidently deciding she had been too familiar, and eager to put their relationship back on its usual footing. 'If you don't mind, I'll bring your breakfast as well. That way, you can take your time. His lordship mentioned that you'd twisted your ankle yesterday afternoon.'

'Yes, I did.'

Francesca looked down at her foot rather ruefully, trying not to resent the fact that Will had mentioned the injury to his staff. She'd like to believe it was because he was concerned about her, but she suspected it was to ensure she stayed where she was until he got back.

'Well, you just take it easy,' advised Mrs Harvey, pausing in the doorway. 'Now, is there anything special you'd like this morning? A nice boiled egg, perhaps?'

'Just toast and coffee, please,' Francesca assured her politely, remaining where she was until the housekeeper had closed the door. She wasn't particularly hungry; she seldom cared what she ate.

But it seemed she was not expected to return to London today, and she was unwillingly aware that her strongest emotion was one of relief. It might not be the wisest thing, staying at the Abbey after what had happened the night before, but that was her problem. Judging by Will's reaction, it was unlikely to happen again.

The morning passed without incident. By the time she had showered and had her breakfast, it was well on the way to lunchtime, and after binding her ankle with an elastic bandage Mrs Harvey had provided for her Francesca made her way downstairs. She felt at liberty to move around the house freely as Will wasn't there, and she even ventured out onto the terrace and leaned on the stone balustrade, admiring the garden below.

She would have liked to walk to the lake, where she knew there was an old gazebo, where she and Will used to watch the sunset many moons ago. But bearing in mind the limitations of her ankle, and the trouble she'd got into the day before walking on her own, she was forced to abandon that idea. Besides, it was possible to see the lake from her position on the terrace, and she realised she'd forgotten how beautiful the Abbey grounds actually were.

The house itself was another story. Turning, she propped her elbows on the stonework at either side of her, and tilted her head back to look up at its ivy-hung façade. It was beautiful, too, but it was beginning to show its age, its crumbling stonework revealing how desperately in need of repair it was.

It was a shame, she thought, that such a beautiful old building should be allowed to decay. With its many leaded windows reflecting the light, and the almost medieval crenellations surrounding its roof, it had an ageless appeal. It wasn't strictly Jacobean; there had been too many extensions and additions for that. Yet it possessed a timeless beauty that couldn't be denied.

Of course, Will's ancestors hadn't been short of money. They hadn't had to contend with taxes and death duties, and labour had been cheap. Will had told her once that his great-great-great-grandfather had spent thousands of pounds installing a ballroom that was never used. His wife had died in a hunting accident, and the 4th Earl had never been seen in company again.

But shortage of money was probably why Will was squiring Emma Merritt around, thought Francesca cynically. It might have been at his grandmother's suggestion, but it seemed he had no objection to the plan. And it wasn't as if it would be any hardship marrying Miss Merritt. Francesca remembered all too clearly how very attractive that young woman was.

She had lunch in the morning room, where she and Will had had breakfast the day before. There was consommé, and pasta, with a delicious bowl of chocolate-flavoured rice pudding to finish, and although she hadn't felt particularly hungry when she'd sat down she managed to eat everything that was put before her.

'We'll soon have you feeling your old self again,'

remarked Mrs Harvey, serving the coffee herself, and Francesca wondered what 'old self' that was: the comparative innocent she'd been before she'd married Will, or the shattered woman he'd left her. She pondered. These days, it was hard to remember anything in between.

She was standing in the drawing room, considering the doubtful advantages of either scanning one of the magazines about country life that were strewn on small tables around the room or going up to her apartments to rest, when she heard a car pull up outside. Going to the window, she saw an ancient Rolls-Royce sitting on the drive, and even as she stood there, transfixed, she saw Will's grandmother being handed out of the back seat by her chauffeur.

A mixture of emotions swept over Francesca at that moment, not the least of which was panic. But it didn't last long. Recent experiences had made her tougher, and she doubted that anything Lady Rosemary had to say would hurt her now.

All the same, it required some stamina to remain where she was when every instinct inside her was bidding her to flee. Will wasn't here; she had no need to see the old woman. She could leave it to Mrs Harvey to tell their guest that she was resting in her room.

But on the heels of this thought came the realisation that, of course, Lady Rosemary hadn't come to see Will. She knew he was out, and therefore her visit here had nothing to do with him. Francesca supposed she should have expected it. As soon as Will had told her he'd informed his grandmother that she was here, she should have known the old witch wouldn't leave her alone. Despite the successful job she'd done in convincing Will that Francesca didn't have a heart, she was evidently wary. She wanted to know what was going on. She wanted to ensure that Francesca wasn't here to resurrect old scores.

Which was why she was still standing gazing with

apparent nonchalance out of the window when Lady
Rosemary came into the room. She'd heard the tap of
the old woman's cane on the hall floor so she was not
entirely surprised at how quickly she had gained admittance to the house. Obviously, she wouldn't stand on
ceremony, although when she turned to look at her old
adversary she saw Watkins hovering anxiously behind
her.

'Can I get you anything, your ladyship?' he asked,
sidling round her to make his request. 'Some tea, perhaps? Or a glass of sherry?'

'Not now, Watkins.' Lady Rosemary dismissed the
old man with a careless flick of her wrist. 'I'll let you
know if I'm staying. Close the door behind you as you
go out.'

Francesca could feel her nerves tightening at this deliberate display of autocracy, but apart from turning to
perch on the cushioned window seat she made no con-
cession to the old woman's presence. On the contrary,
she regarded Will's grandmother with the appearance of
calm authority, and Lady Rosemary looked slightly
taken aback by her apparent indifference.

Still, age had taken its toll of the old woman, and,
clicking her tongue, she crossed to one of the sofas that
faced one another before the hearth and sat down. Then,
legs slightly apart to accommodate her cane, she regarded Francesca with evident irritation, before tilting
her head to speak.

'Why did you come here, Francesca? You must have
known that you wouldn't be welcome.'

Francesca sucked in her breath. As always, Lady
Rosemary had got straight to the point. No prevarication
for her, no hint of cordiality. She'd come here for a
purpose, and she intended to be heard.

'Not welcome?' Francesca said, managing to sound
almost astonished. 'I wouldn't say that. Will was most
insistent that I should stay for the weekend.'

'Will's a fool,' retorted his grandmother curtly. 'It's

not convenient for you to be staying here at all. Particularly not this weekend, when he's got other commitments.' She shook her head. 'He always was too gullible for his own good.'

'Well, I'd agree with you on that,' said Francesca coldly, getting up from the window seat and crossing to rest her trembling hands on the back of the sofa opposite. 'He believes what you say, for one thing. Only someone who was very gullible—or very loyal—would do that.'

Lady Rosemary's lined cheeks suffused with hot colour. 'You can't speak to me like that.'

'Can't I?' Francesca was amazed at her own temerity. She arched her dark eyebrows. 'I believe I just did.' She lifted her shoulders carelessly. 'What can you do about it?' Her lips curled. 'That you haven't already done, of course.'

The old woman's eyes were malevolent. 'Don't underestimate me, Francesca. Just because you're not married to Will any more doesn't mean I can't have an influence on your life. One word from a friend of mine who just happens to be a member of the government, to your employer—Mr Hamishito? Is that right?—and you may find yourself looking for another job.'

Francesca swallowed. 'You're lying.'

'Am I?' Lady Rosemary's gloved hands tightened about her cane. 'Are you prepared to take that chance?'

Francesca's nails dug into the soft leather. The old woman was watching her intently, and it was obvious she thought she had the upper hand. If she gave in to her now, she might as well go back to London. She'd have proved to her how vulnerable she still was.

Francesca took a breath. 'You'd do that?' she said. 'Just to get rid of me?' She shook her head. 'I don't understand. What have you got to fear from me?'

'I don't fear you,' snorted the old woman furiously, but the paper-thin skin beneath her nose was beaded with sweat. 'I don't want you here, Francesca. You're a—

sick woman, and you don't belong here.' Her face contorted. 'You never did.'

'I suppose that's why you made it your business to get rid of me,' suggested Francesca tautly. 'I knew you didn't like me, but I never realised you'd do anything to break up our marriage. Even to the extent of destroying your own great-grandchild. I'd say that was a pretty sick thing to do, wouldn't you?'

Lady Rosemary's nostrils flared. 'I don't know what you're talking about.'

'Of course you don't.' Francesca was contemptuous. 'You'll probably go to your grave denying it, but that doesn't mean it isn't true. You know and I know that I wanted that baby. But that old fool you called a doctor would have done anything you said.'

Lady Rosemary held up her hand. 'If you're talking about Dr Rossiter, you couldn't be more wrong. He's a fine physician. Ask anyone who knows him. He's dealt with our family for over forty years and, not only that, he's a very dear friend.'

Francesca caught her breath. 'You mean he's still practising?'

'Hardly that.' Lady Rosemary rubbed the brass head of her cane with an impatient finger. 'Naturally, he's retired now. From general practice, at least.'

Francesca shook her head disbelievingly. 'He seemed so old,' she said, barely audibly. 'I was sure he must be dead.'

'Well, he's not,' said Will's grandmother shortly. 'He often dines at Mulberry Court. Since his wife's death, it's become his second home.'

'Was that his choice or yours?' asked Francesca caustically. 'I imagine you feel obliged to keep him sweet.'

'I don't feel—obliged to keep him sweet or otherwise,' retorted Lady Rosemary coldly. 'He's an old man. He needs companionship. And he has nobody else.'

'How convenient,' said Francesca ruefully, and once again Will's grandmother showed her contempt.

'He's not incompetent, if that's what you were hoping,' she stated bleakly, her blue eyes glacial. 'So if you were thinking of challenging his capabilities, think again.'

Francesca blew out a breath. 'You know, I hadn't thought of that. Until you brought it up, such a thing had never even entered my head. Is that why you're so desperate to get rid of me? Are you afraid I might repeat my doubts to Will?'

'Don't be ridiculous!' Lady Rosemary stamped her cane on the floor. 'I warn you, Francesca, I won't be thwarted. I want you out of this house tonight.'

Francesca hesitated a moment, and then walked deliberately round the sofa and seated herself opposite the old woman. 'I'm afraid that's not possible,' she said, extending her leg so that the other woman could see the bandage. 'I'm afraid I've had a small accident. I sprained my ankle when I was out walking yesterday afternoon. It's not as painful as it was, but it's still swollen. I couldn't possibly drive all the way back to London tonight.'

Will's grandmother was incensed. 'I don't believe it.'

'It's true.'

'Then my chauffeur can drive you,' Lady Rosemary declared. 'He does little enough for his keep. He'll be glad to take you. I'll get Watkins to ask him to come in.'

'Don't bother.' Francesca stopped her before she reached the bell. 'I brought a friend's car, and I've no intention of leaving until I'm able to drive it back myself.'

Lady Rosemary sank back into her seat. 'You refuse to leave?'

Francesca hoped she wasn't going to regret this. 'Yes.'

'Then you leave me no choice but to contact my friend in London,' said the old woman, getting heavily to her feet again. 'I just hope you know what you're doing. In your situation, I'd have thought you'd want to keep your job.'

Francesca frowned. '*My* situation?'

'Yes.' Lady Rosemary nodded. 'Will told me you were being persecuted by some man. I have to say, it doesn't really surprise me. You always were too provocative for your own good.'

Francesca's jaw dropped. 'Provocative? Me?'

'Yes, you,' said Lady Rosemary tersely. 'I never approved of the way you behaved, the way you dressed. All those short skirts and tight trousers.' She surveyed the younger woman critically. 'And I see you haven't changed at all.'

'Oh, I have.' Francesca remained where she was, but it took an effort. 'And you know it takes all sorts to make a world. You never know, your threats may work to my advantage. If I'm out of work, I've got nothing to go back for.'

'If you think Will will allow you to stay here—'

'He might,' murmured Francesca provokingly. 'Whatever you think, Will still cares about me. If you're not careful, you just might overplay your hand.'

Will's grandmother was breathing shallowly now, and an ominous tide of colour was sweeping up her neck. 'Are you threatening me, girl?'

As if.

Francesca swallowed, suddenly losing her taste for this discussion. She had never threatened anyone, and she wouldn't wish to do so—not even her old enemy.

'No,' she said flatly, rising from the sofa. 'I was just thinking aloud, that's all. Surely you can't object to that?'

Lady Rosemary regarded her with a steely stare. 'But you won't leave?'

'I can't,' said Francesca firmly. 'Not until tomorrow, anyway.'

'Tomorrow.' Will's grandmother tapped her cane on the floor. 'I have your word on that?'

Francesca's lips twisted. 'If that means anything to you,' she said.

'I'll consider it,' declared the old woman curtly, and without even a word of farewell she marched arrogantly to the door.

Francesca was at the window again when the Rolls-Royce pulled away, but Lady Rosemary didn't look back. Francesca could see her, sitting stiffly on the bench seat, much as she'd sat on the sofa moments before. She obviously disdained the use of a seat belt. She was probably of the opinion that no one would dare to run into her car. She rode through the ranks of sightseers, waiting to enter the grounds, with all the hauteur of a *grande dame*.

But when Francesca turned away from the window she found she was shaking. Crossing swords with Will's grandmother had proved far more exhausting than she'd thought. There might have been some small crumb of comfort to be gained from the fact that she'd bested her, but she realised she wasn't half as tough as the old woman imagined she was.

As far as staying on at the Abbey was concerned, that had been pure bravado. Apart from anything else, Will didn't want her here. She shouldn't mistake the way he'd kissed her as anything more than sympathy. The fact that she still found him sexy as hell was her fault, not his.

CHAPTER TEN

WILL arrived home soon after four o'clock. It was earlier than he had anticipated, but the day hadn't been a complete success, and when it had started to rain in the middle of the afternoon Emma hadn't been averse to returning to Mulberry Court.

Whether she had thought he might stay and have tea with his grandmother Will couldn't be certain. As they had been struggling for conversation for the past couple of hours, he hadn't thought she'd be particularly disappointed if he cried off. Surprisingly, the old lady hadn't twisted his arm either, although she had insisted that he join them that evening for supper, as the Merritts were leaving the following day.

He'd wanted to make some excuse, but had known he couldn't. Not without upsetting Lady Rosemary, and giving the Merritts the impression that he wasn't interested in their daughter. The fact that Emma's outrageous comments no longer amused him as much as they had was hardly relevant. He was only meant to marry the girl, for God's sake. Not indulge in intelligent debate.

Nevertheless, he'd left his grandmother's house in a decidedly contentious mood. Six hours of listening to Emma chattering about clothes and holidays, and flirting with him whenever she could, had aroused an acute sense of being used. And his ill humour wasn't improved when he found his ex-wife asleep in the library.

She had evidently been reading a book she had taken from the shelves when exhaustion had got the better of her. And she was curled up in *his* chair, of all places. Her apparent lack of concern for his feelings irritated him like hell.

113

Dammit, he thought, if Francesca hadn't destroyed their relationship, he wouldn't be in the unpleasant position of having to look for a wife. Without that unfortunate experience to cite as an example, his grandmother wouldn't have stood a chance of persuading him to let her take a hand.

The fact that he was also all too aware of the line of midriff exposed by her shirt having come away from the waistband of her jeans didn't help matters. However successful he might have been in rationalising what had happened the night before, the feelings wouldn't go away. He was still attracted to her, he acknowledged bitterly. With the agony of her betrayal losing its sharpness, it was all too easy to remember what might have been.

His fists clenched. He was getting maudlin. And he must be mad even to contemplate going down that road again. He was mistaking her natural fears about the stalker for vulnerability. It was only because she'd needed his support that he'd seen her again.

He was tempted to slam the library door and startle her into wakefulness, but something—some innate sense of compassion, perhaps—persuaded him to use discretion instead of force. Besides, he didn't want her to know how she affected him. So long as she was here, he must keep their association detached from any personal response.

With the door closed, he approached the desk where the book she had been reading was lying, the pages open at no particular place. He picked it up. It was an old copy of *Wuthering Heights* that his father had once bought for his mother. And he guessed the fact that it was set in Yorkshire had influenced her choice.

He flicked it open. He remembered glancing through it when he was a schoolboy, and how he'd harboured a certain sympathy for Heathcliff. Perhaps it had been a case of precognition, he thought wryly. Heathcliff, too, had loved a woman who had effectively destroyed his life, though he wouldn't wish Cathy's fate on Francesca.

Or would he?

He put the book down with rather more violence and the sudden sound pulled her instantly out of sleep. 'Oh, God!' she exclaimed, thrusting her feet to the floor and gazing up at him with wide startled eyes. 'I must stop doing this. It's getting to be a habit.'

Will shrugged. 'You weren't harming anyone,' he declared, ignoring the feelings of resentment he had suffered when he'd first found her here. He pushed his hands into his jacket pockets. 'How's your ankle?'

'Oh—' She glanced down automatically and then, noticing that her shirt was loose, she made an awkward attempt to push it back into her waistband. 'It's much better, thanks. As you'll have gathered, I haven't done anything very energetic today, so it should be all right by tomorrow.'

'Mmm.' Will took a deep breath. Her efforts at restoring her shirt had caused her nipples to pucker, and now her small breasts were clearly outlined beneath the soft fabric. 'You're planning on leaving tomorrow?'

'Of course.' If she was aware of his fascination with her body, she didn't show it. 'I have to go back to work on Monday.'

'And it's not much fun being here on your own?' he suggested, his eyes moving to the neckline of her shirt, and the dusky hollow he could just see above the V. His fingers positively itched to stroke the provocative curve of her throat, and dip inside to thumb those swollen nipples, and it was the devil's own job to keep control of his tongue. 'I'm sorry about today. I'd promised to take Emma to York and show her the Minster.'

'That's all right.' Francesca's lips had stiffened, and he wondered if she'd realised what he was thinking. 'And I haven't been alone—not all day, anyway. Your grandmother paid me a visit.'

Will's sexually induced inertia fled. 'The old lady's

been here?' His hands came out of his pockets, and he thrust irritated fingers through his hair. 'What the hell for?'

Francesca tilted her head to look up at him. 'You didn't know?'

'What?' Will gazed at her with narrowed eyes. 'That Rosie was coming here? Of course not.' He frowned. 'Did she say I did?'

'N-o-o.' Francesca looked down at the desk, tracing the grain of the leather with a thoughtful finger. 'I just wondered, that was all.'

'Well, I didn't,' said Will harshly. 'What did she want?'

Francesca's mouth took on an ironic slant. 'Can't you guess?'

Will scowled. 'Frankly, no. I can't imagine what you and she might have to say to one another.' His scowl deepened, and he came to rest his hands on the desk across from her. 'Unless she was—warning you off.'

'Got it in one.'

Francesca drew back, as if intimidated by his nearness, and, pressing her hands down on the arms of the chair, she got somewhat tentatively to her feet. It reminded Will that, whatever she said, her ankle wasn't cured yet, and he was annoyed to find that this realisation didn't arouse the emotions it should. On the contrary, he knew a sense of relief that he might not have to face his own reactions to her leaving as soon as he'd thought.

'I hope you told her that your staying here has nothing to do with her!' he exclaimed harshly, straightening from the desk and moving so that he was in the path she would have to take if she attempted to come round the desk. 'My God, why can't she mind her own business? What did she hope to achieve by speaking to you?'

'I believe I've just answered that one,' replied Francesca stiffly, wavering a little as the barrier he had created forced her to put most of her weight onto one leg. 'Anyway, it's hardly important, is it? It's not as if she has anything to fear from me.'

Will's dark brows descended. 'That's an odd choice of words,' he observed, and he saw the consternation in her eyes.

'I just meant it's not as if our—current association is in any way personal,' she amended swiftly. 'You know your grandmother never approved of me. Perhaps she just wanted to ensure that I wasn't here to try and resurrect our previous relationship.'

Will's mouth compressed. 'And, of course, you're not.'

'No.'

She was indignant now, and he wondered why her response roused such a sudden sense of irritation in him. But, dammit, she had left here swearing she still loved him. Was it so outrageous to expect that a little of that emotion might have lingered on?

'How can you ask such a thing?' she continued, and he saw that she had interpreted his reaction as something else. 'Unless she—that is, Lady Rosemary—has convinced you I might be lying about that, too.' Her lips twisted. 'I imagine you saw her when you took your girlfriend back to Mulberry Court.'

Will didn't bother to try and deny again that Emma was his girlfriend. After all, if his grandmother had her way, she'd soon be considerably more than that. He was too busy trying to control his own emotions, particularly when Francesca chose to wet her lips in such a provocative way.

Yet he knew she wasn't being deliberately provocative. On the contrary, he was well aware that the only one prolonging this conversation was him. If he got out of her way, she'd be out of the door so fast, he'd stand no chance of stopping her. Injured ankle or not, he sensed that she was as tense as a coiled spring.

'I believe you,' he said at last, rubbing the pad of his finger over the polished surface of the desk at his side.

The wood was smooth, but nowhere near as smooth as her skin, he reflected, watching her with hooded eyes. What would she do if he touched her? Did he really want to find out?

'Then do you mind getting out of my way?' she asked, the tremor in her voice revealing how apprehensive she really was. She put a hand up to her hair, which was scraped back into a tight braid this afternoon, and twined a loosened strand about her finger. 'I'd like to take a bath before supper.'

An image of Francesca in the bath instantly filled his inner vision. Steam rising from sudsy water, long limbs emerging rosy pink or lathered with soap above the rim of the tub. In the past, it hadn't been unknown for them to take a bath together. The ancient plumbing at the Abbey did have some advantages, he recalled...

'Do you mind?'

She was closer now, evidently deciding that she had to take the initiative, or run the risk of exposing how fearful she was. But not of him, he chided himself, remembering what had brought her here. He was confusing her emotions with his, which wasn't the same thing at all.

'Of course.'

He stepped aside then, and he was sure he was just imagining the look of relief that crossed her face. Whatever, she hobbled past him, obviously eager to get away, and he propped his hip against the desk as she hurried out of the room.

It was some minutes later that he remembered he wouldn't be in for supper. Finding Francesca asleep, and then her revelation that his grandmother had been to see her, had emptied his mind of all other considerations, and he gave an exclamation of annoyance. Of course, his own reactions at finding her there hadn't made for rational thinking, but it was irritating to think that he was now going to have to explain where he was going, when it should have been at the forefront of his thoughts.

He had poured himself a drink, and now he emptied his glass and set it down on the desk before leaving the room. He knew he'd probably have left for Mulberry Court again before Francesca came downstairs for the evening meal, so he really had no option but to go upstairs and explain.

Encountering Watkins in the hall outside was not the relief it should have been. Instead of asking him to deliver a message to Mrs Quentin, he merely nodded to the man before continuing on his way upstairs. His jaw compressed. What was he doing? Anyone would think he was looking for an excuse to go to Francesca's room.

Which, of course, he was.

Will acknowledged that fact as he strode along the corridor to his ex-wife's rooms. Just because he had a legitimate reason, that was no excuse for taking advantage of the situation. He didn't honestly know what he wanted of her. Except perhaps a chance to prove to himself, if no one else, that he was no longer the credulous fool he had once been.

He knocked at the door.

There was no response, and he guessed she was probably in the bath. His stomach clenched. What now? Did he dare walk in on her? How would she react if he opened the bathroom door?

He took a breath. This was stupid, he thought irritably. He was behaving like a would-be suitor on a first date. They'd been married, for God's sake. Francesca had no secrets from him. Well, not physical ones, he amended bitterly. He doubted he'd ever been able to understand her mind.

He knocked again, and when there was still no response he opened the door. As he'd expected, the bedroom was empty, but he could hear the sound of running water coming from the bathroom. That was obviously why she hadn't heard his knock or his entrance, he acknowledged tautly. He wondered if she was already in the bath.

He closed the bedroom door behind him, unwilling for anyone else to apprehend his intentions. Indeed, he still wasn't at all convinced of what those intentions were, and as he stood there, looking about him, he had the uneasy feeling that this was a mistake.

He should leave, he thought. He should get outside that door again now, before Francesca realised what was going on. He had no real excuse for invading her privacy. Just because this was his house, that was no reason to behave as if he owned her as well.

But still he stood there, taking in the sight of her jeans and shirt, discarded on the age-scarred ottoman that stood at the end of the bed, of her make-up case open on the dressing table, and the tantalising scent of the perfume that she wore. Everything she owned was so completely feminine. It was that that kept him there— that compulsive reminder of his own masculinity.

He moved towards the dressing table, picking up an atomiser of perfumed deodorant and raising it to his face. He sniffed and the unforgettable fragrance filled his nostrils, bringing back memories that he'd believed were long forgotten. But they weren't. The poignancy of the visions they evoked made him dizzy with longing, and he thrust the container back onto the cut-glass tray and started for the door.

Behind him, he heard the bathroom door open, and he realised with a feeling of humiliation that the water had stopped running. Francesca must have heard the chink of glass on glass, and there was no way now he was going to get out of there without an explanation.

'Who's there?'

Her startled cry brought him to an immediate halt, and although it was the last thing he wanted to do he had no choice but to turn and face her. Schooling his features into a mask of apology, he slowly reversed his position.

'I just remembered—' he was beginning, when he caught sight of her shocked face and realised, with a pang of shame, that he had frightened her. But even that thought was swiftly overtaken by his reaction to her appearance. He'd been prepared to find her in a bathrobe, a towel even, but what he found was something infinitely more disturbing than that. He was sure the lacy bra and matching panties were far more provocative than her nude body would have been, her hair loose about her shoulders and framing her unnaturally pale face.

'Will!' She swallowed, and he was ruefully reminded that she was totally unaware of his feelings. Unaware, too, of her own semi-nudity, he guessed, as she struggled to come to terms with what was real and what was imagined. 'Oh, God, I thought—I thought someone had broken in.'

'Sorry.' He endeavoured to sound sympathetic, when every nerve in his body was scraped raw with other emotions. 'I shouldn't have come in. I was looking for a piece of paper. I was going to leave you a note.'

Liar!

'A note?'

She looked confused, and no wonder, he mused bitterly. 'To explain that I won't be in to supper this evening,' he went on doggedly. 'I forgot to mention it earlier. I'm dining at Mulberry Court.'

'Ah!' She licked her lips now, and as if his prosaic announcement had brought her down to earth she passed a nervous hand over her midriff. 'Well—that's all right. There's no need for you to explain your movements to me.'

Will's lips tightened. 'I know that,' he said, resenting the implication. 'I just thought I ought to—warn you, that's all.'

'Warn me?'

'That you'll be eating alone,' declared Will shortly. He straightened his spine. 'It seemed the decent thing to do.'

'Did it?' Suddenly she didn't seem as vulnerable as she'd seemed before. 'Are you sure about that?'

'Am I sure about what?'

'Well...' She lifted her slim shoulders and he had to force himself not to watch the narrow strap that slipped down her arm and exposed the upper curve of her breast to his fascinated gaze. 'You weren't entertaining the thought of taking up where you left off last night by any chance?'

'No!' The denial exploded from him. The fact that that thought had been in his mind made her accusation that much more damning to him. 'I've told you why I came. I wanted to explain the situation. You flatter yourself if you think I had any ulterior motive at all.'

'Perhaps.' But she didn't sound convinced. 'So—what are you waiting for?'

'What am I—?' He scowled. 'What are you talking about?'

'Well, you have delivered your message,' she pointed out softly, rubbing the palms of her hands up and down her bare arms. 'Don't let me keep you. You must want to get ready for your date.'

Will's teeth clenched. 'I don't have a date.'

'Whatever.' She shrugged. 'I'm sure she'll be more receptive than me.'

'More grateful, at least,' he snapped, tempted beyond all reason. 'May I remind you I didn't invite you here?'

Francesca seemed to soften. 'I know,' she said, looking a little unhappy now. 'I'm sorry. You've been— great.' She took a few tentative steps towards him, and then faltered. 'I do appreciate it. It's just—hard to remember how things used to be.'

Will's body tensed. Hell, he thought, what did she think he was made of? Lead? Already his mind was beyond the point of stripping those sexy garments from her, and his palms were damp with sweat.

'Fran—' he began, but she didn't let him finish.

Which was just as well, he assured himself later, not sure what he had been about to say. Something foolish, no doubt, something he'd be sure to regret afterwards.

He'd been thinking with his sex at that moment, not with his head.

'I want you to be happy,' she murmured as the haze before his eyes began to subside. 'I'm sure—Emma won't let you down.'

Will groped for the door, and wrenched it open. Not until he was safely outside in the corridor, with the door closed firmly behind him, did he let the breath out of his lungs. Then he gave in to the urge to collapse weakly against the wall, and wonder how in God's name he was going to let her go...

CHAPTER ELEVEN

FRANCESCA left before Will was up the next morning.

It was a deliberate decision on her part, and she had spent part of the previous evening finding out where Smedley had parked Clare's car. She'd already known it was in the garages somewhere, and a damp stroll in the grounds after supper had elicited the information that although the car was under cover the garages were seldom locked.

Which had suited her purposes admirably, and although she'd been tired she'd slept only shallowly, half afraid she might lose her advantage. Consequently, she was up at six o'clock, writing Will a note, thanking him for his hospitality and assuring him that she felt much more capable of coping with her problems now. She also wished him luck for the future, firmly suppressing any hint of bitterness and expressing the hope that he found what he was looking for. Or what his grandmother was looking for, she amended to herself, with rather less charity.

At that hour of the morning, the motorway was fairly quiet, and despite some discomfort from her ankle she made good time on the journey south. It was only a little after half past nine when she turned into Harmsworth Gardens, and, ignoring the anxiety that stirred in her stomach when she saw Number 29, she drove purposefully into the courtyard.

She only glanced up at the windows of her flat, although she was instantly aware of the undrawn curtains, and, turning off the engine, she pushed open her door. She'd just tossed her bags on the back seat of the coupé

so now she leaned in to get them before locking the car
and starting rather stiffly towards the house.

Mrs Bernstein met her at the door. 'Oh, Francesca!'
she exclaimed. 'You're back. Are you all right?'

'I'm fine,' said Francesca, edging past her. She wasn't
really in the mood for a chat with her landlady, and she
had hoped to gain the sanctuary of her flat as anony-
mously as she'd left the Abbey.

'Gary fixed your window,' went on Mrs Bernstein,
apparently unaware of her tenant's desire to get away.
'He did it on Friday morning, before he went to work.'

'That was kind of him.' Francesca was grateful, although she wished she hadn't had to be reminded of the
reasons why she'd fled the flat in the first place. 'Please
thank him for me, won't you?'

'Of course I will.' Mrs Bernstein regarded her with
some concern. 'You went to Yorkshire, did you?'

'That's right.' Francesca bit her lip. 'I spent the weekend with—with an old friend. I just drove back this
morning.'

'All the way from Yorkshire?' Mrs Bernstein was impressed. But then anywhere north of Watford might as
well have been another planet so far as she was concerned. 'No wonder you look tired.'

'Oh, do I?' Francesca felt a momentary trace of humour. Trust Mrs Bernstein not to pull her punches. 'Yes,
well—I probably need a rest.'

'Probably,' agreed the landlady, and then, as
Francesca was starting ruefully for the stairs, the older
woman let out a cry and called her back.

'Honestly,' she said. 'I'd forget my head if it was
loose.'

'Why?' Francesca's heart sank. 'Nothing else has happened, has it?'

'Well, that depends how you look at it, I suppose,'
said Mrs Bernstein confidentially. 'That young police-
man, Sergeant Cameron, came looking for you.'

'For me?' Francesca could have groaned. She'd only

been back five minutes, and already she was tired of the subject. She was particularly tired of talking to policemen. It seemed that short of hiring herself a bodyguard there was little they or anyone else could do. 'What did he want?'

'He didn't tell me,' said Mrs Bernstein, shaking her head. 'But I think it was something urgent. He told me to ask you to give him a ring as soon as you got back.' She paused. 'Do you think they've caught him?'

Francesca swallowed. 'Who? The stalker?' She gave a mirthless little laugh. 'I doubt it.'

'Well, you will ring him, won't you?' persisted Mrs Bernstein anxiously. 'I shouldn't like him to think I hadn't given you the message.'

'I'll ring him,' Francesca assured her, wearily beginning to climb the stairs. 'And thanks. For everything.'

Although she was vaguely apprehensive about entering the flat, she knew at once that no one had been there in her absence. The air was still, the atmosphere inside the apartment still retained a trace of the perfume she invariably wore, and the film of dust on the furniture revealed no fingermarks at all. Perhaps he'd seen her leave, she thought uneasily. Even though he hadn't followed her, he might still have been aware that she was away. The blinking light on the answering machine might give her an answer, but she waited until she'd made herself a cup of coffee before she faced that fear.

To her relief, however, the only messages left for her were from Tom Radley. He had called on Friday, before he'd left for work, before she had had the chance to explain her whereabouts to him. He'd sounded worried, and she realised she should have warned him she was going away. No wonder he had been impatient when she'd called him from the Abbey.

A glance into the fridge reminded her that apart from anything else she had little food in the apartment. The bread she had left from Thursday was stale, and the fruit in the fridge was already sprouting patches of mould.

She'd have to call at the mini market, but she could do that on her way back from Clare's. She needed to return her friend's car, but first she had to ring Sergeant Cameron.

The sergeant wasn't in. His deputy explained that he was out on a call, but that he'd be available later in the day. He suggested that instead of calling she might like to come down to the station at about two o'clock. That way, she could be sure of seeing him, and save herself a journey later.

Francesca didn't understand the latter half of the message. She couldn't imagine why the police sergeant should want her to go down to the station in the first place, but she kept her doubts to herself. Unless they'd decided she'd been making it up, she reflected bitterly. Perhaps they were going to charge her with wasting the police's time.

It was just something else to worry about, and with a heavy heart she unpacked her bags and set the washing machine in motion. Then, after checking the bathroom window, which had been repaired, as Mrs Bernstein had said, she grabbed her bag and left the flat.

Clare was still in her dressing gown when she arrived at her house. Francesca kept forgetting it was Sunday morning. Since she'd got back, she seemed to have forgotten what day it was. Still, her friend was endearingly glad to see her, insisting that she come in and have some breakfast when she discovered Francesca hadn't eaten since the night before.

Clare's husband, Mick, was already seated at the kitchen table, ploughing his way through a huge plate of bacon, eggs and sausage. As usual these days, he was wearing the vest and sweatpants he wore to go to the gym, and Francesca guessed he'd be working out there later, probably to compensate for the amount of food he was shovelling into his mouth now.

'Sit down, Fran,' invited Clare, giving her husband an impatient look. 'Don't mind Mick. He's a pig, and he knows it.' She met his indignant stare with a defiant look. 'He'll be leaving soon, won't you, lover? What time did you say you were going to the gym?'

'Why?' Mick regarded Francesca consideringly. 'So you two can talk dirty behind my back?'

'Don't be stupid, Mick!' Clare was angry now, and she frowned at him darkly. 'I don't think remarks like that are appropriate at the moment, do you?'

'Oh, yes. The phantom stalker!' Mick pulled a wry face, and resumed eating the food. 'Did you find anything out about the broken window?' He chuckled. 'He's a cocky bastard, isn't he? You have to give him that.'

'I know what I'd like to give him,' retorted Clare, shaking her head apologetically at Francesca. 'Now, what would you like, Fran? A bacon sarnie, perhaps?'

'Just toast, thanks,' said Francesca quickly, avoiding Mick's mocking stare. 'And as a matter of fact I think there must have been some developments. The police sergeant who interviewed me before wants me to go down to the station this afternoon.'

Mick looked up now. 'What for?' he asked, ignoring his wife's warning nudge to his shoulder. 'What did he say? Have they found out who he is?'

'I don't know...'

'In any case, it's nothing to do with us, Mick,' said Clare reprovingly. 'I doubt if Fran wants to talk about it just now.' She busied herself at the stove. 'Tea or coffee? Mick has coffee, but I prefer tea myself.'

'Coffee for me, please,' replied Francesca, not entirely averse to Mick's enquiry. 'And I have no idea what it's all about. I wish I did. I wish they had caught him. I'd like to think the creep was behind bars.'

'Hmm.' Mick chewed thoughtfully. 'Well, that's typical, isn't it? The police ask you to go and see them, but don't bother to tell you why. If you ask me, they haven't got a clue about anything. If they had, they'd have caught the bloke by now.'

'Yes.' Francesca couldn't help but agree. In the last

six months they'd achieved absolutely nothing. 'Thanks,' she added as Clare handed her a plate containing two slices of toast. 'I don't think I'll be able to eat all this.'

Clare shook her head, and seated herself beside her husband. 'Well, do your best,' she said, spreading butter on a slice of toast for herself. 'Now, tell me about your weekend. That's much more interesting. Did you do anything exciting? What is—Will doing these days?'

'Will,' scoffed Mick disparagingly. 'He's the ex-husband, right? The lord of the manor, no less.' He grimaced. 'I bet he wasn't pleased when you turned up on his doorstep.'

'What do you know about it?' exclaimed Clare, elbowing him in the ribs. She looked at Francesca and pulled a face. 'Sorry again, Fran. Take no notice of Mick. He's just jealous, that's all.'

'Jealous!'

Mick was resentful, but his wife had little sympathy for him. 'Yes, jealous,' she said firmly. 'Since you lost your job, you can't bear the thought that other people are successful. If you spent more time down at the job centre, instead of in front of the television, you might find something useful to do.'

Mick's chair crashed back against the kitchen cabinet. 'You rotten bitch!' he said angrily, glaring at his wife. 'I don't have to listen to this.'

'No, you don't,' she said complacently. 'You can go down to the club, as usual, and stop being so nosy. I know you're only hanging on because you're hoping to hear some gossip you can pass on to your drinking cronies.'

Mick's face twisted. 'One of these days, Clare,' he said, but his wife waved him off with a careless hand.

'Save it,' she said. 'I've heard it all before.' She took a sip of her tea. 'Lunch will be on the table at two o'clock. I know you won't be late. The big match starts at three.'

Mick slammed out, and for a few moments there was an uncomfortable silence in the room. Francesca didn't like the thought that she had been the cause of friction between her friend and her husband, and she half wished she'd just delivered the car and not come in.

Then Clare pulled a wry face. 'Sorry about that,' she said, reaching for the teapot. 'Mick's always grumpy in the mornings.'

Francesca expelled a breath. 'Weren't you a little hard on him?' she ventured, not liking Mick Callaghan particularly, but wanting to be fair, and Clare grimaced.

'He deserved it,' she said, without compassion. 'He can be such a jerk.' She shrugged. 'But by the time he's pumped some iron, and swallowed a few pints of bitter, he'll have forgotten all about it.'

Francesca wasn't convinced, but she didn't say anything. Who was she to pass judgment on anyone's marriage? She hadn't made such a success of her own. But she didn't want to think of that. It was too painful. It was hard enough to give Clare an edited account of her weekend.

She left Clare's house about eleven, walking back to Harmsworth Gardens through a fine drizzle. Clare had offered to drive her, but Francesca had explained that she wanted to call at the mini market, and it was only a few yards from there to the flat.

All the same, she kept a wary eye out for strangers as she walked the quarter mile between the two buildings. It was funny, she thought. While she had been in Yorkshire, she hadn't felt as if she was constantly under surveillance. It might be partly psychological, as the police had suggested, but the feeling was back again, and she was overwhelmingly glad when she reached her flat.

The washer had switched off in her absence, and she was transferring the clothes to the dryer when the phone began to ring. Immediately, her throat dried and her palms began to sweat, and she got to her feet rather shakily. But when the answering machine picked up she realised it was Will.

'Fran?' he said. 'Fran, are you there? If you are, dammit, answer me. At least let me know that you're all right.'

Leaving the clothes hanging out of the washer, Francesca reluctantly crossed the small sitting room to the phone. The kitchen was only separated from the living area by a breakfast bar, so she hadn't far to go. 'I'm here,' she said huskily, picking up the receiver, and she heard him give a relieved sigh.

'Thank God,' he said, his tone sharp with concern. 'I think you might at least have had the decency to let me know what you were planning to do.'

'I couldn't,' murmured Francesca unhappily, aware of how achingly familiar his voice sounded. Faced with the choice, she doubted she'd have had the strength to make the break, particularly if he'd tried to persuade her to wait for a few more days. 'I thought it was better this way.'

'Better for whom?' asked Will tersely, his anger showing through. 'Goddammit, Fran, we never did talk about what you were going to do when you got back.'

'There's not much I can do,' she averred, not wanting to discuss her fears with him. Not now; not after she'd burned her bridges. Whatever happened now, she was on her own.

'Well, was the flat okay?' he demanded. 'You haven't had any uninvited visitors while you've been away?'

'I don't think so.' But, in spite of herself, Francesca shivered. The truth was, would she ever know?

'You don't think so?'

Will's tone mirrored his impatience with her now, and she hastened to assure him that everything was fine. In fact, she could have said that leaving him had been the hardest thing to do. She'd had her anger to sustain her five years ago. This time, there was just an empty sense of grief.

'So, how's your ankle?'

'My ankle?' Francesca looked automatically down at her foot, and pulled a face. 'Well,' she admitted, 'it is a bit stiff after driving all the way from Yorkshire, but I can walk on it, if that's what you mean.' She took a breath, and then went on, 'I—I am grateful to you, Will. For—for letting me use the Abbey as a hotel.'

Will blew out a breath. 'And that's all?'

Francesca was confused. 'What else is there?'

'Well, you could say you enjoyed seeing me again.'

Francesca swallowed. 'Well, I did.' She stopped herself there, before she said something she shouldn't. 'Um—have you told your grandmother I've gone?'

'Not yet,' he retorted, his tone hardening. 'It's got nothing to do with her. I meant what I said yesterday: the old lady does not run my life.'

Doesn't she?

Francesca thought the words, but didn't say them. Making rude comments about Lady Rosemary wouldn't do her any good now. And, whatever Will said, he was still the 9th Earl of Lingard, and his grandmother would never let him forget it.

'Anyway,' he continued, when she didn't comment, 'I'm coming down to London myself in a few days. I may look you up. Just to make sure that you're all right,' he added, the irony evident in his voice. 'I wouldn't want you to think I had any ulterior motive.'

Francesca's breath caught in the back of her throat. 'I wouldn't do that,' she said hurriedly. 'I don't know what I'll be doing, when I'll be home.' She didn't think she could survive another parting.

'Then I'll just have to take my chances, won't I?' he remarked, but she could hear the edge of anger in his voice. 'Take care, Fran. I'll be thinking of you.'

And he rang off.

CHAPTER TWELVE

IT WAS after eight when Francesca got home, and she was exhausted. She hadn't been sleeping well for months, and since she'd got back from Yorkshire the situation hadn't improved. She had thought that once she was back in London she'd be able to get her feelings for Will into perspective, but it hadn't happened. Instead, they only seemed to have got stronger, disrupting her days and destroying her nights.

Of course, the news that the police sergeant had been waiting to convey should have eased her mind, but it hadn't. The fact that they'd arrested a man who had been caught breaking into the adjoining apartment building and, under interrogation, he had confessed to being her stalker seemed just too convenient to be true. The man was a habitual criminal, with any number of previous offences, and according to Sergeant Cameron he wasn't entirely right in the head.

She acknowledged that he might have tried to break into her flat; that it might have been he who broke her bathroom window. But he'd looked nothing like the man she'd seen outside her apartment, even if the police had suggested it was she, and not they, who had made a mistake.

And naturally they'd been delighted to clear the matter up, as the sergeant had put it. They had no jurisdiction as yet for arresting a stalker, but the man's confession had killed two birds with one stone. It was easy in the circumstances to find excuses for keeping the man remanded in custody. The amount of stolen goods found at his home was only a start.

If Francesca found some loopholes in their reasoning,

no one wanted to hear them. A quantity of drugs had been found as well, and the man had been charged. Another reason for not placing too high a priority on his memory of the phone calls, Sergeant Cameron had insisted. The man was a loner. He probably followed women because it gave him a cheap thrill.

But still Francesca wasn't entirely convinced. If it didn't sound so outrageous, she'd have said the man was merely seeking notoriety for a change. He was an addict, and a thief, she had to accept that. But being a stalker was something else.

She'd said as much to Clare just yesterday.

She and her friend had been having lunch in the staff canteen when Tom Radley had appeared and asked if he could join them. It was the first time Clare had actually met Tom. They worked in different departments at Teniko, and Francesca could tell at once that she wasn't impressed.

But she'd offered no objections to Tom joining them, and it had been during the course of their discussion that Francesca's doubts had come to light. In fact, it was the first time she had actually admitted them to herself. Until then, she'd pretended to believe what she'd been told.

In fact, she'd been gazing blankly into space when Clare had attracted her attention. 'Hello,' she said, leaning across the table towards her. 'I said, what did Hamishito bawl you out about this morning? I saw him go stamping out of the department. He asked me about some studies you were supposed to have prepared for him last Friday.'

Francesca's shoulders sagged. 'Oh, it was just a preliminary study I was supposed to do for him.' She scowled. 'I haven't even finished collating the figures yet.' She pushed aside the sandwich she had bought for her lunch, and rested her forearms on the table. 'He's a slave-driver, that man. Do you know, he hasn't even asked if I'm better?'

'You've not been ill,' pointed out Tom drily, and Francesca gave him a defensive look.

'He doesn't know that,' she declared. 'As far as he's concerned, I was suffering from a gastric infection. The least he could have done was ask me how I was.'

'Perhaps he thinks you look all right,' remarked Tom carelessly, displaying the lack of sympathy he'd shown since she'd refused to reconsider his offer to stay at the flat. 'If you ask me, it was all a storm in a teacup anyway. You said yourself you haven't heard a squeak from that creep since you got back.'

'Well, that's because he's in prison,' said Clare, defending her friend loyally. 'He can hardly terrorise her from his cell, can he?' She tossed her head. 'Why do men always think they know best?'

'I don't believe I—'

'I'm not sure he is in prison,' Francesca interrupted Tom quickly, speaking her thoughts for the first time and earning a look of disbelief from Clare. 'I'm not,' she insisted unhappily. 'That man they've caught—I don't think he's the one.'

Clare snorted. 'That's not what you said before.'

'I know.' Francesca slumped in her seat. 'But I'm afraid they've made a mistake. I know he confessed to—to everything, but I think he's still out there.'

Tom frowned. 'But you don't know that.'

'No.' Francesca caught her lower lip between her teeth. 'But I feel it. Oh, God!' She buried her face in her hands. 'I must be getting paranoid. I can still feel his eyes on me.'

Clare sighed, and as if the look she exchanged with Tom said volumes he finished his tea and got abruptly to his feet. 'I'd better go,' he said awkwardly. 'I promised Bob Davis I wouldn't be long.' He patted Francesca's shoulder in passing. 'I'll see you later. If you want me, you know where I am.'

'Thanks.'

Francesca tilted her head back and gave him a grateful

smile, but after he had gone Clare moved her chair a little nearer to her friend's. 'You don't think—' She coloured. 'What I mean is, it couldn't be Tom, could it? You said he'd been really offhand since you turned down his offer to stay at the flat.'

'Tom!' Francesca gasped. 'The stalker!' She gave the other woman a horrified look. 'You can't be serious!'

'Why not?' Clare was defensive now. 'You have to admit he's hooked on you. And it would account for the eyes you say you can still feel on you.'

'I didn't mean now, at this minute,' protested Francesca vehemently. 'I just meant— Oh, I don't know what I meant really. But last night, when I was going home, I got that same creepy feeling. I half expected him to have left a message on the machine.'

'But he hadn't.'

'No.'

'And he hasn't left any messages all week?'

'No.'

'So, that must prove something.'

'Perhaps.' Francesca was doubtful. 'I just wish I could feel convinced. I guess it's going to take a little time to come to terms with it, that's all.'

'Well, it must be him,' said Clare fiercely. 'Who else would admit to doing such a thing?'

'Search me,' said Francesca wearily. 'Perhaps that's how he gets his kicks. Or maybe he thinks it's the only way to make his name.'

Clare had assured her that she was sure the man in custody must be the stalker, but Francesca felt no real sense of security as she let herself into the flat. Despite the fact that, as Clare had said, she had lived a whole week without suffering any kind of harassment, she was wary. She couldn't believe it was all over. Not as simply as that.

It was still a relief to find that the answering machine wasn't winking at her in the shadows, and that the flat looked exactly as she had left it that morning. Maybe she was exaggerating her fears, she thought; maybe coming back to the loneliness of the flat after spending several nights at the Abbey was partly to blame. At Lingard, she'd always been aware of other people around her. At the flat, she was alone, and that did make a difference.

She locked and bolted the door, and then, kicking off her shoes, she padded across the carpeted floor to the bedroom. It was still light enough to see what she was doing, and, shedding her suit and blouse onto a chair, she went into the bathroom and turned on the taps.

A bath first, and then supper, she thought. And perhaps she'd be extravagant and open a bottle of Chardonnay. It seemed so long since she'd been able to relax for a whole evening. She owed it to herself to try and reshape her life.

She had bathed and changed into a lime satin robe, and was in the process of opening the wine, when someone knocked at her door. The sound startled her, and her hand slipped off the corkscrew, sending the bottle flying, but thankfully onto the living room carpet and not the kitchen tiles.

Not that the safety of the wine was of any concern to her at that moment. Indeed, the fact that she scrambled for the bottle was purely to provide her with a means of self defence. She could always smash the bottle, she told herself, shutting her mind to the images of the injuries broken glass could cause. It would be easier for an intruder to take a knife from her than the jagged neck of a bottle.

But that was all hypothetical, anyway, she chided herself, moving reluctantly into the small foyer. It was probably Mrs Bernstein, or one of the other tenants, wanting to borrow a cup of sugar. She was jumping to conclusions, just because night was drawing in.

But Mrs Bernstein went to bingo on Friday evenings, she remembered apprehensively as the knock was repeated. Whoever it was should have phoned first. Her friends all knew the kind of pressure she had been under.

'Fran!' The voice was low and male, and for a moment the blood froze in her veins. Then, 'Fran,' he called again. 'Are you in there? It's only me: Tom. Can I come in?'

The breath surged out of Francesca's lungs in a noisy rush. Tom, she thought dazedly. What on earth was Tom doing here? She'd never invited him to the flat before, and although she knew he knew where she lived she'd never have expected him to be so presumptuous. He had no right frightening her like this. However honourable his motives might be.

And then what Clare had suggested came back to haunt her. How well did she really know Tom? She'd had a drink with him a couple of times, and he'd offered to sleep at the flat to keep her company, but that was that. In fact, apart from knowing he wasn't married, she knew very little about him. Just because he was a colleague, that was no real reason to assume he wasn't involved.

But then common sense prevailed. For God's sake, she thought impatiently, she really would have to take herself in hand. Did she really believe that Tom might be her stalker? He was a friend; she'd worked with him for over three years. She could trust him.

Besides, the man who had been terrorising her was presently residing in a prison cell. Wasn't he?

'Just a minute,' she called now, relieved to find that her voice sounded almost normal. She set the bottle down on the kitchen counter, and tied the belt of her robe more securely. She would have liked to get dressed, but she hoped this wouldn't take long. 'I'm coming,' she added, and walked firmly into the foyer.

'Did I disturb you?' he asked when she opened the door, and Francesca bit her lip. She thought it must be blatantly obvious that he had, bearing in mind her state of undress, and the tumbled disorder of her damp hair. But this was Tom, she reminded herself. He was only being polite. She hoped he wouldn't expect her to invite him in.

'That's all right,' she said, forcing a smile. 'This is a surprise, Tom. You should have phoned. I might have been out.'

Had he hoped she would be?

'It was a spur-of-the-moment thing,' he replied, looking beyond her into the flat. 'I thought you might be glad of the company.'

Francesca took a deep breath. 'Well, that was kind of you, Tom, but—'

'I'm intruding?'

He looked so charmingly innocent standing there that Francesca felt a reluctant sense of shame. 'I—not exactly,' she said, smoothing a hand over her midriff. 'But—I wasn't expecting visitors, as you can see.'

'That's all right.' Tom was obviously not going to leave without being told to do so. 'You and I don't have to stand on ceremony, do we?' He pulled a hopeful face. 'Aren't you going to invite me in?'

Francesca hesitated. 'Well—if you'll wait until I get dressed—'

'No problem.' Tom stepped forward, and she had to let him into the foyer. 'But don't bother about me, Fran. I won't be staying long.'

There was nothing for it but to close the door and follow him into her living room. Short of ordering him to leave, and making things difficult at work, she had no choice. Besides, she told herself fiercely, she could handle this. She was letting her apprehension about the stalker colour her life.

'Um—sit down,' she said, gesturing towards the sofa. 'I was just about to have a glass of wine. Perhaps you'd like to join me?'

He could have a glass of wine, and then she'd get rid of him, she decided firmly. She could always plead a headache. That was a good standby.

'Sounds good to me,' said Tom, but he remained on

his feet and accompanied her into the tiny kitchenette. 'Hey, let me do that,' he added, when she picked up the corkscrew again. 'Hmm—Chardonnay. My favourite.'

'Is it?'

Francesca wished she didn't find that so hard to believe. But on the odd occasions when they'd had a drink together he'd always chosen beer, and she'd never heard him mention wine before.

But what did she know?

'Oh, sure,' he said now, winding the screw down into the bottle. She noticed he did it rather inexpertly, managing to leave half the cork in the bottle, but he scooped it out with the handle of a spoon, and Francesca pretended not to notice.

'So,' she said, when the wine was poured, and she had put a more comfortable distance between them, 'I didn't expect to see you tonight.'

'No.' Tom waited until she had perched herself on the arm of the sofa before taking the seat nearest to her. 'But, after what you said yesterday lunchtime, I was concerned about you.'

Francesca suppressed the urge to move again, and gave a rueful smile. 'Well, that's very kind of you,' she said, 'but you don't have to worry about me. In any case, I've come to the conclusion I must be wrong. The man—the man the police have in custody is—is *him*.'

'Your stalker?'

'The man who was stalking me,' amended Francesca carefully. 'Yes.' She moistened her dry lips. 'It's such a relief to—to know it's all over.'

Tom frowned. 'You think it is?'

Francesca nodded. 'Most definitely.'

Tom looked puzzled. 'But you seemed so sure it wasn't him yesterday.' He paused. 'Has something happened to change your mind?'

Francesca could sit still no longer. 'It's the time factor, you see,' she said, swallowing a generous mouthful of wine, and moving to the other side of the room. 'It's been a week now since—since he phoned me. A week since the bathroom window was broken. It can't be just a coincidence, can it?'

Tom shrugged. 'I suppose not.'

'You sound doubtful.' Francesca gazed at him nervously. 'You were fairly disparaging about it yesterday.'

'That was before I had had time to really think about it,' declared Tom, getting up from the sofa and following her across the room. 'Now I'm not so convinced a man like that would just confess his guilt to the police. Why would he? Why should he? He was already in custody. What did he have to gain?'

Francesca felt cornered. She could hardly move away from him again without it looking as if she was trying to avoid him. But the longer this conversation went on, the more anxious she became. And, although she didn't really give any credit to what Clare had said, the fact remained she was alone here with a man she hardly knew.

'I'd really rather not talk about it,' she said now, finishing her wine, and holding the glass with both hands, like a shield. 'Um—was that the only reason you came?'

'Not entirely.' Tom took her empty glass from her unresisting fingers and placed it, with his own, on the nearby bookcase. 'I also came to apologise for yesterday. I was an unsympathetic devil. I'm sorry.'

'Oh, that's—' Francesca was beginning, when he reached out and trailed his hand down her sleeve.

'I like your robe,' he said thickly, fingering the silky fabric. 'It's soft, and smooth, and sleek—just like you.'

Francesca panicked. There was no other way to describe the emotion that gripped her at that moment. His coming here was so unexpected, and she was already in a state of nerves. When he touched her, when he stroked her robe, she saw it as an invasion; when he spoke in that soft—and menacing?—voice, she heard it as a threat.

Even so, the way she jerked away from him, the way

she scurried across the room, was childish. She was behaving as if she'd never been alone with a man before.
But his startled, 'For God's sake, Fran!' only quickened
her footsteps, and, jerking open the outer door, she practically fell into the arms of the man who was standing
outside.

The scream she had been suppressing escaped then,
and for a mindless moment she was convinced he must
have an accomplice. But then Will's familiar—if savage—voice brought her to her senses, and she collapsed
against him weakly, unable to speak.

'What the hell's going on?' Will demanded, his arms
closing about her with protective strength. He dipped his
head towards her, his warm breath fanning her hot temple. 'For God's sake, Fran, if anyone's touched you—'

'They haven't.' It was Tom who spoke, opening the
door wider and gazing at them both with obvious distress. 'For heaven's sake, Fran, surely you know I'd
never hurt you? I was only trying to show you I cared.'

'Were you?' It was Will who answered him, stepping
into the foyer and successfully blocking his escape. 'I
asked what was going on,' he reminded them. 'Who is
this man, Fran? Did you invite him here?'

Francesca groaned, and pulled herself together. If she
wasn't careful, Will and Tom would be at one another's
throats. 'It's Tom,' she said, drawing away from him.
'Tom Radley. You remember, I told you he was a friend
from where I work.'

'Radley.' Will said the man's name, but it was hardly
a greeting. His eyes seemed to register Francesca's state
of undress, and they narrowed. 'Do I take it, then, that
you did invite him here?'

'That's not the point,' broke in Tom, evidently aware
of where this was leading. 'I'm a friend of Fran's, as
she says.' He squared his shoulders. 'There's been a mis-
understanding, that's all. Who are you?'

'I'm her husband,' said Will curtly, apparently forgetting the fact that they were divorced. His eyes dark-

ened as they rested on his ex-wife, and she sensed his displeasure. 'And you haven't answered my question, Fran. Did you invite him here?'

Francesca sighed. 'I—no.' She met Tom's defensive gaze, and wavered. 'Not exactly.'

Will's brows arched. 'What is that supposed to mean?'

'It means—Tom called round on the off-chance.' She bit her lip. 'To see if I wanted to go for a drink.'

Will's expression barely altered. 'Really?'

'Yes, really,' put in Tom, grateful for the let-out. 'I'm sorry. I seem to have got the wrong signals.'

'What signals are you talking about?' asked Will, his voice icy. He stepped past Francesca, and pushed his face close to the other man's. 'Do you want to explain?'

'I—'

'Just go, Tom,' said Francesca, grabbing his arm and pulling him towards the door. 'I'll see you on Monday, right?'

Will swayed back on his heels as she ushered the other man out of the flat. She knew he resented her interference, but she couldn't let Tom take all the blame. She had overreacted. She realised that now. She didn't know what she'd imagined he was going to do to her when he'd touched her robe.

With the door closed behind Tom, she felt a little more in control, and, walking past Will, she led the way into the living room of the flat. He'd never been here before, and she looked about her rather anxiously. She wanted him to get a good impression. She didn't want him to think she lived in a dump.

She saw the two glasses standing on the bookcase as Will did. Turning her back on them deliberately, she wrapped her arms about her waist. 'So you found me,' she said, desperate to lighten the situation. 'What do you think of the flat? The rooms are fairly small compared to the Abbey, but it's quite cosy, don't you think?'

CHAPTER THIRTEEN

WILL halted in the middle of the floor. He was dressed in black this evening—black jeans, black leather jerkin, black shirt—and Francesca thought how much his clothes fitted his mood. His expression was black, too, black and accusing, and she resented his assumption—unvoiced, as yet, but implicit in his bearing—that she'd brought what had happened on herself.

'So you did invite him here,' was all he said, and she stared at him angrily. How dared he behave as if she owed him some loyalty, when he was probably cutting a swathe through the females his grandmother was providing for him like a hot knife through butter?

'If I did, that's my business,' she retorted. But then honesty forced her to at least attempt to explain. 'I—didn't invite him, as it happens.' She glanced down at her satin robe. 'As a matter of fact, I'd just got out of the bath.'

'But you had no qualms about letting him in,' observed Will caustically, his eyes taking in her tumbled hair. 'I'm supposed to believe you were just passing the time of day, with two empty glasses on the bookcase, and you looking as if you've just got out of bed!'

Francesca gasped. 'You can believe what you like. It's nothing to do with you.'

'Isn't it?' Will's mouth twisted. 'I got the impression you were pretty pleased to see me a few minutes ago.'

'Well, I was—I am—oh—' She lifted her arms and pushed her hands through her hair. 'Stop looking at me like that, Will. If you must know, I didn't want to let him into the flat.'

'So why did you?'

'I don't know.' She turned away. 'He—when he first knocked, I was—frightened. I wasn't expecting anyone, and when I found out it was him I was so relieved—'

'Because of the stalker? It didn't cross your mind that good old Tom might be the stalker?'

'No.' She was defensive. 'Besides, he's been arrested.'

'Who's been arrested?'

'The stalker, of course.' She cast him a defiant look over her shoulder. 'Well, at least a man was caught breaking into the building next door, and he's confessed to being him.' She shrugged. 'Who knows? They could be wrong.'

Will moved towards her. 'Run that by me again. You say the stalker's been arrested, and you didn't bother to let me know?'

Francesca swallowed. 'Well, I—I didn't think you'd be interested,' she said defensively, knowing that wasn't why she hadn't been in touch with him at all. 'I suppose I should have.' She shrugged. 'Sorry.'

'Bullshit!' Will stopped right behind her, and the heat of his breath practically seared her neck. 'You knew I was worried about you, and you deliberately withheld that information for some sick reason of your own—'

'No.'

'Yes.' He grasped her arm, and swung her round to face him. 'And then you have the nerve to tell me you were scared when Radley knocked at your door.'

'I was.'

'Why?' His lips twisted. 'Is he in the habit of coming round here and scaring you, or are you used to having would-be lovers attempt to rape you in your own living room?'

Francesca gulped, and before she could control herself she had raised her free hand and struck him squarely across his lean, sarcastic face. 'You bastard!' she choked, the words coming on the heels of the slap, as if in justification for her violence, but the look in Will's eyes silenced her.

'Bastard, am I?' he asked, in an ominously soft voice, and she had to force herself not to panic as his hand came up and gripped the nape of her neck. 'And what are you, Fran?' he enquired, his thumb digging into the soft flesh behind her ear. 'A cheat? A tease? Or some innocent lamb, caught in a snare of her own making?'

A pulse was beating at his jawline, highlighting the red marks her fingers had made, and for all her apprehension she knew an absurd desire to smooth those marks away with her lips. Even his hand at her nape had a sensuous allurement, and as he continued to look at her she could feel her resistance melting, her limbs dissolving like perspiration on the heated surface of her skin.

'You don't understand...' she got out unsteadily, but when her eyes returned to his face she knew it was too late for explanations.

'Wrong, Fran,' he said huskily, using his hand behind her head to propel her nearer. 'You know exactly what you're doing, and I, poor fool, can't do anything about it.' And, stifling an oath, he buried his face in her hair.

She trembled, but she didn't draw back. The muscled strength of his body felt so good against hers, her breasts crushed against his chest, her limbs entwining with his as he parted his legs to keep his balance. It was enough to find herself in his arms again, and when she felt his lips against her neck she lifted her shoulder in unguarded delight.

'This is madness,' he muttered as his lips moved up her neck, his teeth capturing her earlobe before he deposited a moist kiss behind her ear. 'Are you trying to drive me out of my head?'

'Whatever,' she got out breathily, in no state to conduct a serious conversation, and he groaned before moving on to her mouth.

Hot, sweet passion flooded through her when his lips

found hers. Her mouth quivered, opened, invited the powerful invasion of his tongue. She couldn't seem to get close enough to him, and when she lifted one leg to wind it about his calf he groaned in unwilling protest.

'Can you feel what you're doing to me?' he murmured, as her pelvis pressed intimately close to him, and she expelled a soft sigh.

'It would be difficult not to,' she confessed against his cheek, pushing his jacket off his shoulders so that it fell on the floor behind him. She found one of his taut nipples through the silk of his shirt, and gently bit it. 'I know what you're doing to me.'

'And what's that?' he asked, tracing the contours of her earlobe with his tongue.

'Oh—you know,' she accused him tremulously, and his shudder of awareness rippled through her, as well.

His mouth moved down her throat, parting her robe as he did so, and uttering a sound of approval when he found she was nude beneath it. The two sides fell apart and her small breasts puckered invitingly. They were already dark and engorged with blood, and he took one swollen nipple into his mouth.

His tongue caressed that sensitive peak, rubbing backwards and forwards with such insistence, she was sure her knees were about to give way. The buckle of Will's belt was digging into her stomach and his arousal was hard against her abdomen, too. She closed her eyes and put her hand down between their two bodies, and felt the throbbing heat of his erection. It pulsed beneath her hand, strong and male and insistent, and she rubbed herself against him with sensual intent.

'God!' Will's reaction was swift and immediate, and his hoarse, 'For pity's sake, Fran,' was more exciting than any declaration of his feelings would have been. It spoke of his need, his hunger, and gave her an incredible sense of power that she fully intended to exploit.

His lips found hers again, more urgently now, an unguarded roughness in the way he took possession of her mouth. His tongue plunged between her teeth, imitating the grinding pressure of his hips, and despite herself she sagged against his greater strength.

'I want you,' he said against her mouth, as if she had been in any doubt of it, and her whispered, 'I know,' was more than enough encouragement.

'Is it through there?'

Her mindless needs made it difficult to answer him, but when she nodded he swung her up into his arms and carried her into her bedroom. Her clothes were still strewn about the floor where she had left them, but he kicked them aside. With an agreeable lack of ceremony, he turned on the beside lamp, before depositing her on the mattress, tearing off his own shirt before flinging himself down beside her.

'Better?' he breathed, weighing one delicious breast in his hand and caressing its distended tip with his thumb. His breathing quickened. 'Now I can look at you.' He dipped his head, and found the dusky hollow of her navel. 'I want to watch you while I make love to you,' he added, exploring the sensitive cavity with his tongue.

Francesca was trembling so much, she couldn't think straight. With his dark head cradled against her stomach, she couldn't think of anything but him. His head moved lower, seeking the fiery curls that guarded her femininity, and she shook violently when he pressed his face into the softness there.

'Oh, God, Will,' she moaned, feeling the flooding warmth of her own arousal, and as if her yearning cry was the final straw his fingers sought his belt. Panting with the heat of his emotions, he tore open his zip, and thrust down his jeans and pants. Then, with undisguised urgency, he moved between her legs.

The heat of him touched her, the hardness of his erection pressing intimately into her sheath. It was so long since he had possessed her, and her pride wouldn't let her admit that there had been no one else. In conse-

quence, just for a moment, she resisted him, her muscles
tensing automatically at the unfamiliarity of the act. She
wanted to be cool, but she couldn't do it. Even though
this was exactly where she wanted to be.

'Relax,' he whispered against her mouth, and the sensitive brush of his tongue was enough.

'I am relaxed,' she said, and she suddenly was. The
whole pulsating length of him slid into her, fitting her
so tightly she caught her breath. She remembered how
good they had always been together, how unbelievably
satisfying it was.

'Oh, Fran,' he muttered, his breath escaping on a
strangled sigh, 'I wanted to make this last. But I can't.'
He shuddered. 'If I move, it will all be over.'

'It's all right,' she assured him huskily, drawing his
hand to where their bodies were joined. 'Just—just touch
me there. That's all I need.' She gasped. 'Oh, yes, Will.
Do it!' She took a trembling breath. 'Do it now!'

Francesca realised she must have fallen asleep for a few
minutes, because when she next opened her eyes Will
was lying on his stomach beside her, watching her. And
immediately she remembered what had happened, a
memory that couldn't help but bring the hot colour surg-
ing into her face.

'What—what time is it?' she exclaimed, struggling up
onto her elbows and trying to bring the clock into focus.
It was only then that she realised she was as naked as
he was, and although he had once known her body as
intimately as his own she was still uneasy at finding
herself this way.

'It's early yet,' Will reassured her as she strove to pull
the quilt over her. He pressed her back against the pillows with a firm hand on her shoulder. 'It's barely half
past nine,' he added as she subsided. 'And you have to
admit this is a nicer way to wake up, don't you think?'

Francesca wet her lips. 'Than on the riverbank, do you

mean?' she ventured, trying to be as casual about her nudity as he was, and he gave her a lazy smile.

'Or sitting in my chair in the library,' he agreed huskily. 'I suppose we could have used the desk, but it wouldn't have been half as comfortable.'

Francesca's colour deepened. 'Now I know you're trying to embarrass me,' she said, starting when he bent to bestow a sensuous kiss on her shoulder. She heaved a sigh. 'You never did tell me how you came to be outside my door.'

Will lifted one hand to stroke her breast, his fingertips gliding from the soft slope of her throat to the hard peak that jutted against his palm. 'Do you really need me to tell you?' he asked, replacing his fingertips with his tongue. 'How about if we leave the talking until later? Right now, I've got other things on my mind.'

Francesca swallowed. 'I—I don't think this is very sensible,' she said, struggling to hold onto her composure. 'Will, why have you come to London? I bet your grandmother doesn't expect you to come and see me.'

Will's eyes darkened in the lamplight. In the artificial light his eyes gleamed like polished ebony. 'Like I said,' he breathed, 'let's not spoil things with unnecessary conversation. We're not at Lingard now.' His fingers strayed down over her flat stomach. 'I didn't touch you then.'

Francesca drew an unsteady breath. 'And did you want to?'

'All the time,' he assured her thickly, moving so that one of his legs now lay between hers. He rubbed his hairy thigh against the moist tenderness he had created. 'You know,' he added, against her cheek, 'I get the feeling you wanted it, too.'

'No, I—' Things were getting out of hand again, and Francesca knew she had to pull herself together. It was all very well excusing what had happened on the grounds that she had been disconcerted by his appearance, but she had to remember his intentions were not hers. 'Will!' She turned her head to avoid his searching mouth. 'Is—is Emma with you?'

His growl of impatience was instantaneous. She had used the girl's name deliberately, and the decreasing pressure against her thigh proved that she had chosen wisely. 'No, dammit,' he swore, 'Emma is *not* with me. If it means anything to you, I probably won't be seeing that young woman again.'

'No?'

Francesca suppressed the surge of satisfaction that swelled inside her, but when Will rolled onto his back she saw that she had only partially achieved her other objective. Will was still aroused, albeit with anger, and she despised herself for the sudden impulse she had to take him into her mouth.

'No,' he repeated harshly, slanting a savage look in her direction. 'And if this is intended to remind me of my responsibilities, forget it. I get enough of that from Rosie herself.'

Francesca's tongue circled her upper lip. 'You—you have to admit that—that it's not very—very sensible, though.'

'Sensible?' His lip curled. 'Sensible for whom?'

'Well—for both of us,' she said firmly, taking advantage of his brooding introspection to attempt to slide off the bed. No matter how much she wanted to stay with him, she had to be practical. Giving in to him again would be madness, and she knew it.

But he was too fast for her. As she inched towards the edge of the mattress, he captured her wrist in a lethal grip, and in one lithe movement he rolled over and imprisoned her beneath his muscled weight.

'Don't go,' he said, and the husky appeal in his voice was almost her undoing. She so badly wanted to feel that wild release.

Certainly, it was an attractive option. She wanted him. Oh, God, she thought, how much! But wanting led to needing, and needing Will was something she had al-

ready had to get out of her system. She couldn't do it
again, couldn't bear the thought of their eventual parting,
and that was why she had to convince him she meant
what she said.

'I must,' she said now, closing her eyes against the
sensuality she could see in his gaze. 'Let me go, Will.
You've got what you came for. Now I want to get up.'

The oath he uttered was ugly, but somehow—she
didn't quite know how—she had hit a nerve, and he
rolled off her. By the time she came out of the bathroom,
he had gone, and she was left with the depressing conviction that the only person she had really hurt was herself...

CHAPTER FOURTEEN

CLARE didn't come into work on Monday morning. Her husband rang to say she was full of cold, and although Francesca wasn't really in the mood to commiserate with anyone she felt obliged to call at her friend's house on her way home that evening.

For her part, she had had a miserable weekend, and although she had thought—hoped?—that Will might ring she had been disappointed. Evidently he had taken what she had said to heart, and although it was painful she had to believe she had done the right thing. Apart from anything else, he still believed she had been responsible for aborting their baby, and that old woman, his grandmother, would never let him forget it.

Clare's husband answered the door to her ring, pulling a sardonic face when he saw who it was. 'She is ill, you know,' he said, stepping back to allow Francesca into the hall. 'You didn't have to come and check up on her.'

'I'm not here to check up on her,' protested Francesca, not quite knowing if he was serious or not, and Mick shrugged.

'Looks like it to me,' he remarked, closing the door behind her. 'What's the matter? Has the big bad wolf been chasing Goldilocks again?'

'Goldilocks wasn't chased by the big bad wolf,' Francesca retorted shortly. 'But if you mean have I had any more unpleasant experiences, then the answer is no. The man's behind bars.'

'Yes.' Mick looked thoughtful. 'That's what Clare said.' He grimaced. 'Lucky you!'

'I'd hardly call it lucky,' Francesca was saying defensively, when Clare's nasal tones reached them from up-stairs.

'Who is it, Mick?' she called thickly, and he went to the bottom of the stairs.

'It's your boss,' he answered, with deliberate malice. 'Are you decent? Shall I send her up?'

'Of course she can come up!' Clare exclaimed, some-what croakily, and after Francesca had braved Mick's challenging stare and reached the top of the stairs she called out, 'I'm in the spare room, Fran. Mick's afraid he'll get my germs.'

'Stop moaning!' Francesca had been uncomfortably aware of Clare's husband behind her, and now he fol-lowed her into the small bedroom. Or rather he propped his bulk in the doorway, regarding his wife and her friend with some resentment. 'I don't see why I should listen to you coughing all night.'

Clare ignored him. 'Thanks for coming, Fran,' she said, pointing to a chair near the foot of the bed. 'Sit down for a minute. Unless you're afraid you'll get in-fected, too.'

Francesca subsided into the chair, giving her friend a sympathetic look. 'How are you?' she asked. 'Have you got everything you need? Colds can be the pits if you don't look after yourself.'

'Hey, I'm here,' said Mick, glaring across at her. 'If Clare needs anything, that's up to me. Are you implying I'm not looking after her, or what?'

Francesca was taken aback. 'Of course not,' she pro-tested. 'But if there's anything I can do I'd like to help.' She grimaced at Clare. 'I wouldn't mind a few days in bed myself,' she added ruefully. 'This has definitely been one of those days.'

'Hamishito?' asked Clare, understanding, and Francesca nodded.

'Hamishito—and Tom!' She pulled a face. 'Between them, I feel like a punchball. I'm beginning to wonder if I'm cut out for this job.'

'Tom?' said Clare in surprise, and pulled another tissue out of the box to blow her nose. 'I thought you and Tom—well, that you got on well together. You certainly gave that impression the other day.'

'That was then.' Francesca spoke feelingly at first, and then realised she couldn't tell her friend what had really happened. 'He—well, he's so—insensitive. He always wants to know what's going on.'

'Who's Tom?'

It was Mick who spoke, and Francesca looked up with some embarrassment. She'd forgotten he was there, and although what they were talking about wasn't private she didn't like having to explain herself to him.

'He's a colleague,' she said at last, and as if sensing her friend's unease Clare addressed her husband herself.

'Don't you have anything better to do?' she asked, sniffing resentfully. 'You haven't wanted to keep me company all day.'

'That's because it's boring sitting up here listening to you snuffling into a tissue,' retorted Mick unfeelingly. 'This is much more interesting. If Fran's got a love life, I'd like to know.'

'Tom's not my lover!' exclaimed Francesca indignantly. 'I've told you, he's just a friend.'

'And in any case she's still in love with her ex-husband,' declared Clare, with a warning grimace. And then, at her friend's startled look, she said, 'I'm sorry, Fran. It just seems so obvious to me.'

'Clare—'

'Her ex-husband!' Mick was disparaging now. 'Well, that's a lost cause if ever I heard one. According to Clare, he's already found himself a replacement. I know that name—Merritt. Isn't her father into computers or something?'

'Shut up, Mick.'

Clare was red-faced now, and Francesca realised her friend had probably told her husband everything she'd told her. She ought to have expected it, she supposed, but somehow she hadn't. And it hurt to think that Mick Callaghan might have been laughing at her behind her back.

'As—as a matter of fact, I saw Will on Friday,' she said, as much to wipe the smug look off his face as from any real desire to confide in her friend. She licked her lips. 'He was in London, and he came to the flat for the evening.' She felt the guilty heat in her cheeks, but ignored it. 'He—it was—good to see him again.'

Clare's red-rimmed eyes were wide. 'Crikey,' she said. 'So he wasn't quite as indifferent as you thought.'

'Oh, I—' Francesca couldn't have her thinking that, so, in spite of Mick's sneer, she hurried to amend that impression. 'I—no. It was just a—friendly visit. I don't expect I'll be seeing him again.'

Will drove away from the Abbey with a feeling of burning his bridges behind him. No matter what happened now, he was going against everything he'd believed for the last five years, and if he lived to regret it, so be it.

And he would live to regret it—or so his grandmother would say when she found out. She didn't know what he was doing, of course, but when she did he had no doubts about what her reaction would be. And she might be right; he might be making the biggest mistake of his life. But somehow that kind of logic no longer applied.

He was probably all kinds of a fool, he reflected, not without a trace of bitterness. He was passing up the opportunity to solve all his financial problems in one fell swoop for—for what? His lips twisted. For a woman who had never wanted children; who had cared more for her career than for him.

And yet, if what Francesca had always claimed was true, she had wanted their baby. She hadn't been responsible for miscarrying their child. So what? It had been an accident? A spontaneous abortion? Such things were possible, were commonplace, in fact. And if his grandmother hadn't come up with that story about

Francesca visiting some sterile abortion clinic in Leeds he'd never have suspected it was anything else.

But old Archie Rossiter had confirmed it. He'd admitted that Francesca had asked him if he couldn't get rid of the foetus, and when he'd refused she'd evidently found someone else who would.

Will's stomach clenched. Even now, even after all these years, the injustice of what had happened caught him on the raw. Five years ago, Francesca had given him a choice: believe her, or believe his grandmother and Archie Rossiter; and because he'd secretly suspected that she hadn't wanted the baby he'd made his decision. But had it been the right decision? He doubted he would ever know.

The fact was, if he still wanted Francesca—and, God help him, he knew he did—he had to put the past behind him. He had to believe her story, or spend the rest of his life living a lie. He had only ever loved one woman; he suspected he always would. And that was more important than anything else.

He reached Kensington soon after six o'clock, and rather than telegraph his arrival by parking in the forecourt of the Victorian apartment house he found a space in the next street. Then he sat for a few moments gathering his thoughts before venturing into Harmsworth Gardens.

God, he thought, he hoped she'd be pleased to see him. He was investing so much in this visit, and he had no real proof that she would want to see him again. Just because she had let him make love to her, that was no reason to assume that she wanted to rekindle their relationship. On the contrary, just four days ago, she had asked him to get out of her flat, and persuading her that she should give him another chance was not going to be easy.

He sighed.

And that was without the inevitable confrontation there would be with his grandmother if he did succeed in bringing Francesca back to Lingard. Francesca's feelings towards the old lady hadn't mellowed with the years, and there was no doubt in his mind that Lady Rosemary hadn't forgiven her for what she thought she had done.

He frowned. Could Archie have been wrong? Could he be the real culprit here? Perhaps Francesca hadn't wanted the baby at first, and perhaps she'd confided her feelings to the old man. Was that why, when she'd miscarried, Archie had immediately assumed the worst?

Of course Francesca had blamed the old doctor for what had happened, but no one had believed that he could have done anything wrong. For God's sake, he had been caring for pregnant women and delivering their babies for years. She had been clutching at straws, that was all, and if he had any hope of their getting together again he had to accept that she hadn't been entirely rational at that time. She'd needed someone to blame, and she'd blamed him.

But what if Archie had done the same?

Will folded his forearms on the wheel and rested his chin on them. Whatever, he had to dispel the ghosts of past transgressions, and persuade Francesca to do the same. Surely, if his grandmother saw how happy they were together, she would understand. But if not... He heaved a sigh. He cared for his grandmother; of course he did. She had practically brought him up, after all. But if it came to a choice between her and Francesca... He pulled a rueful face. There was no contest.

Deciding he had been sitting there long enough, Will pulled the keys out of the ignition and thrust open his door. He hadn't brought any luggage with him, just his shaving gear and a change of clothes stuffed into a duffel bag which he left in the Range Rover. There was no point in pushing his luck, he thought ruefully. Francesca was just as likely to send him away.

He saw her car turning into the courtyard of Number 29 as he reached the corner; saw, too, the nondescript

Ford that pulled away at his approach. If he hadn't known better, he'd have said that the man in the car had been watching her from across Harmsworth Gardens, and although the thought didn't linger he was glad Francesca wasn't going to be alone tonight.

Or, at least, he hoped not, he acknowledged, reaching the gates of the house just as Francesca got out of her car. He paused by the gates, aware that as yet she hadn't seen him, feeling his senses stirring as she reached into the back of the car for her briefcase.

Suddenly, she became aware of him.

As she was drawing back, she seemed to sense his presence, and he was sorry he had stopped to watch her then. She jerked back, banging her head on the roof of the car as she did so, and he realised immediately what she'd thought.

Of course recognition was almost instantaneous, and her breathless exclamation was not polite. Then, when she was able to speak, she rounded on him. 'What the hell do you think you're doing?' she demanded hotly. 'Are you spying on me as well?'

'No.' Will stifled the urge to answer in kind, realising she had some justification for her anger. 'I've just got here, as it happens.' He frowned, remembering the car. 'You're not saying you think you're being followed again?'

'Of course not.' She was impatient at his suggestion, and he had to accept that he was wholly to blame. 'In any case, you didn't answer my question. If you've come for a repeat performance you can think again.'

'I haven't.' Will took a deep breath. 'But I do want to talk to you. Can I come in?'

She hesitated, and he wondered dully what he would do if she refused. He'd had such high hopes on the way here, but now he felt he'd blown it. Frightening her had not been part of his plan.

'I can't think what we have to say to one another, Will,' she declared at last, which was neither a yes nor a no, and he saw how she was chewing on her lip after she'd said her piece. It might just be wishful thinking, but he got the feeling she wasn't entirely averse to seeing him, even if her words belied his thoughts.

'Well, I don't intend to talk out here,' he said at last, taking a chance. He pushed his hands into his jacket pockets. 'You could at least offer me a drink.'

'I only have wine,' she muttered rashly, and Will hid the satisfied expression that crossed his face.

'I like wine,' he said softly. 'You know that. Does that mean you're going to let me in?'

Francesca pressed her lips together. 'I suppose so,' she replied offhandedly, slamming the car door and activating the alarm. 'But I've got work to do this evening,' she added, indicating the briefcase. 'Clare is off at the moment, so I'm filling in.'

'Clare?' Will considered. 'Oh, yes, that's your friend. The one who lent you her car.' He touched the bonnet of the small Peugeot in passing. 'I must say, I like your choice better than hers.'

Francesca made no comment, leading the way into the building without a backward glance. It was left to Will to follow her, and to try and keep his eyes off her long legs as she climbed the stairs ahead of him. She looked so sexy in a suit, he thought. But then, in his opinion, Francesca looked sexy in anything.

She had some trouble getting her key into the lock when they reached her door, but he doubted it was because he was making her nervous. On the contrary, despite the way he'd startled her downstairs, she seemed totally controlled now. She wasn't relaxed, that was true, but he sensed that was because she didn't trust his motives for being here.

There was one of those free newspapers lying on the floor just inside the door and Francesca bent to pick it up before walking into the foyer. Will was treated to a tantalising view of her bottom, taut beneath the navy linen of her short skirt, and he had to clench his fists to prevent himself from gripping her hips and pulling her back against him. It would have been so easy to do it; so easy to forget why he was here. But it was not the way to gain her trust, and he turned to close the door.

There was a scrap of paper caught in the letterbox. At first, he thought it had been torn off the newspaper she had carried through to the living room, but it didn't feel like newsprint and he turned it over. There were three words printed on the other side, and a wave of almost blinding fury swept over him as he read them. He closed his eyes for a moment, willing the adrenaline pumping through his veins to subside. Then he stuffed the piece of paper into his pocket and followed her into the other room.

'Something wrong?'

Ever vigilant, she had observed his change of mood, and Will made a concerted effort to put a smile back on his face. 'What could be wrong?' he countered. He glanced around. 'You said something about a glass of wine. I hope it's not the same bottle you were sharing with Radley the other night.'

Francesca pursed her lips. 'I poured the rest of that away after you'd gone,' she said pointedly, dropping her bag and briefcase on a chair and walking into the small kitchen. She opened the door of the fridge. 'I've got a German white or a German white,' she added, hefting one of the two bottles in her hand. 'I'm sure you'd prefer French wine but I don't have any.'

'Who cares, as long as it's cold?' responded Will, regaining a little of his equilibrium and coming to rest his palms on the breakfast bar. He watched her take two glasses from the cupboard, and the corkscrew from the drawer. 'Did you have a good weekend?' He paused. 'After I'd gone, of course.'

Francesca hesitated. She didn't like lying to him. He could tell that. But, equally, she had no intention of making it easy for him. And, while she studied, he was struck by something significant. Francesca had never lied to him before.

Not even about losing the baby?

'I had a—pleasant weekend,' she said eventually, taking the cork out of the wine bottle with a satisfying pop.

'And—you've not had any more trouble—' Will broke off, and then continued steadfastly, 'With the stalker, I mean? I gather you've had no more phone calls since—since he was caught.'

'No.' Francesca poured wine into both glasses with only a faint tremor in her wrist. 'Drink up,' she added crisply, returning the bottle to the fridge. 'I've not got all night.'

'And I have?' suggested Will drily, trying to put all thoughts of the message he had intercepted out of his mind. Anyone could have pushed that piece of paper through her letterbox, he assured himself firmly. The delivery boy, a copycat criminal—anyone. If the man was in prison, she had nothing to worry about, so thank God he'd found it and not her.

'Well, have you?' she queried now, picking up her glass and folding her arms across her midriff. 'Why have you come, Will? What is it you want to say to me? If it's an apology, then forget it. I warn you, I'm not in the mood for your lies.'

'It's not an apology,' said Will flatly, leaving his glass on the counter and turning to rest his hips against the bar. 'And I haven't told you any lies, as far as I'm aware.'

'Haven't you?' She didn't sound convinced. 'You said you weren't going to see Emma Merritt again.'

'I'm not.' He was confused, but she merely arched a mocking brow.

'Then why are you in London? I assumed her family had a place in town.'

'I came to see you.' Will watched the effect his words had on her. 'I know it's hard for you to believe, but I want us to start again.'

Francesca caught her breath. 'Start again?' she echoed. 'Will, I told you before we came upstairs—'

'I'm not talking about what happened on Friday night,' he declared mildly, and she thrust her glass down on the counter beside his with an unsteady hand.

'That's good,' she said tersely, her eyes flashing with indignant fire. 'Because I don't intend to have sex with you again.'

Will sighed. 'It wasn't sex, Fran—'

She snorted. 'Wasn't it?'

'No.' His eyes softened as they rested on her face, which was animated now with her emotions. 'We loved each other on Friday night, Fran. We made love, and that's a wholly different thing.'

Francesca took a step back. 'So we loved each other on Friday night, did we?' she taunted, doing her best to sound facetious. 'But not on Saturday morning, right? That was a whole different story.'

Will shook his head. 'That's not what I meant.'

'Isn't it?' She obviously thought she was winning the war of words.

'No.' Will crossed his arms to prevent himself from reaching for her. 'I love you, Fran. There's no time limit on it. And I want you to come and live with me again.'

Her consternation would have been laughable if it hadn't meant so much to him, and, feeling in need of some sustenance, he twisted round and took a drink out of his glass. The wine was palatable, but it was no substitute for whisky, and he had to steel himself not to empty the glass.

'You want—what?' she got out at last, obviously having a problem with articulation, and Will took a deep breath before he spoke.

'I want you to come back to live at Lingard,' he said. 'I want us to be together. I want the chance for us to start again.'

Francesca's throat worked convulsively. 'You—you're not serious.'

'I'm afraid I am.'

The colour rose up her neck. 'But—until a couple of weeks ago you never expected to see me again.'

'I know.' His tone was gentle. 'I guess I don't deserve for you to listen to me. But maybe the way it happened was fate. Who knows?'

Francesca swallowed again. 'I don't believe you said that.'

'Why not?' His face was serious. 'Stranger things have happened.' He paused. 'Whatever it costs, I want you. I don't care if you believe me now. I'll prove it to you, if you'll let me. And—' he put out a hand and trailed his fingers down her sleeve '—I don't think you'll regret it if you do.'

Francesca backed away from him. 'This is crazy!'

'Why is it crazy?'

'Because—because if you'd really loved me you'd never have let me go.'

'That cuts both ways,' said Will drily. 'You walked out on me, Fran. All right, I didn't try to stop you, but if you'd stayed we could have worked it out.'

She halted. 'I'd lost my baby, Will!'

'I'd lost a child, too,' he reminded her steadily.

'Yes. But you weren't being accused of getting—getting rid of it, were you?' Her voice broke uncontrollably. 'You wouldn't listen to my story. You'd made up your mind that I was lying, and that was that.'

Will groaned. 'I know.' He lifted both hands to rake back his hair. 'But you have to try and understand how I felt. I'd been told—well, you know what I'd been told—and I was hurting, dammit. I realise now that the old man must have made a mistake, but back then I wasn't thinking too clearly about anything.'

Francesca stared at him. 'Is that what your grandmother's told you?' She caught her breath. 'Is that why you're here—because that old woman has decided to cover her back?'

'To cover her back?' Will didn't know what she was

talking about. 'Fran, I'm here because I love you. That's all.'

'But she knows you're here?'

'No one knows I'm here,' replied Will flatly. He blew out a breath. 'Does it matter? We loved each other then.' He hesitated. 'I believe we still do, or I wouldn't be here.'

'You wish.' But there were tears in Francesca's eyes now, and he badly wanted to take her in his arms. 'You do realise that—that, however we feel, your grandmother will never allow this.' Her breath caught in her throat. 'She still hates me. She always will.'

'Oh, Fran.' Will sighed and came towards her, and although she tried to get out of his way the wall was at her back. Putting one hand on the wall at either side of her head, he stood looking down at her. 'Forget Rosie,' he said huskily. 'She doesn't matter to us.'

'She does.' Francesca's hands were flat against the wall, too, her chest rising and falling rapidly with the tumult of her breathing. 'She does hate me, Will. I tried to tell you before. She always has. I still believe that she got Dr Rossiter to—to terminate my pregnancy.'

Will regarded her despairingly. 'Oh, Fran, don't ask me to accept that my own grandmother would do a thing like that. She hurt you; I know that. She hurt us both. But don't let her—her jealousy come between us again. I'm admitting I was wrong. I shouldn't have listened to her distortions. I know you wouldn't have destroyed our baby. I should never have accused you of such a thing.'

Francesca darted a look up at him. 'You believe I didn't do anything to bring on the miscarriage?'

'Yes.' Will brought one hand to stroke her cheek. 'I must have been crazy to even contemplate such a suggestion. I guess I needed to blame someone. I'm not proud to admit it, but I guess I chose you.'

'Because your grandmother told you that that was what had happened.'

'All right.' He was prepared to concede that the old

lady had put the thought in his head. She had certainly given him Archie Rossiter's version of the facts as he knew them. He could only assume a terrible mistake had been made. 'Look,' he said now, 'can't we put the past behind us? For good? We've got this chance to start again. Can't we take it?' He brushed her mouth with his. 'Please.'

Francesca wouldn't look at him. She continued to stare at a point level with his tie, and as he watched a fat tear rolled unhindered down her cheek. He didn't know what to say, what he could say to comfort her that hadn't already been said. He loved her, he wanted her, he *needed* her in his life.

'Your grandmother never thought I was good enough for you,' she said at last, and he closed his eyes against the conviction in her voice. 'She told me—more than once—that she didn't expect the marriage to last.' She paused. 'She wanted you to marry someone grander, someone with money. You know how much she wants the Abbey to be restored.'

'Mmm.'

Will regarded her with troubled eyes. It was true enough, he supposed. The old lady had always had something of an obsession with the Abbey. It had been her girlhood home, and Will was sure it had been a great wrench when she had had to leave. But the entail had meant that her brother had inherited the place on their father's death, and when she'd got married she'd moved to Mulberry Court.

Not that that had been the end of her connection to Lingard, he remembered thoughtfully. In the fullness of time, her daughter had married her cousin, Will's father, and when his parents were killed her grandson had become the 9th Earl. The fact that she had also been made his guardian must have been a source of some satisfaction to her. For a while, at least, she'd been in total control.

But loving something and being prepared to do anything to maintain it were two entirely different things, he assured himself fiercely. All right. The old lady hadn't liked Francesca, but he'd never allowed her feelings to come between him and his wife. And as far as he knew she'd accepted his choice without further argument. To hear that she'd expressed her doubts to Francesca took some believing even now.

'You never said anything!' he exclaimed, trying to come to terms with what Francesca had told him, and she expelled a rueful breath.

'No,' she agreed. 'No, I didn't. If I say I didn't want to hurt you, will you believe me?' She shrugged her slim shoulders. 'I didn't care what she said to me. So long as you loved me, that was all I cared about.'

Will cupped her face in his hands. 'I do love you. I always have. Even when you went away, and I told myself I hated you for what had happened, it wasn't true.' He smoothed his thumbs across her cheekbones. 'You were always there, inside me, making every other woman I met seem second-best.'

Francesca looked up at him now. 'Do you mean that?'

'Of course, I mean it.'

'And—the other?'

'Rosie, you mean?' His lips twisted. 'Well, I will admit she is fairly fanatical about the Abbey.'

In fact, he brooded unwillingly, he wouldn't have thought of getting married again if it hadn't been for his grandmother. But the old lady was so determined that Lingard should stay in the family, that he should have a son, so that it wasn't handed on to some distant relative, just because he happened to be male.

'You don't believe me, do you?' Francesca said suddenly. She lifted her hands to his chest, in an attempt to push him away. 'You'll always wonder if I was lying. Oh, God, Will, just let me go!'

'I can't,' he said simply, taking her resisting hands behind his back. 'And you're wrong; I do believe you.' He paused. 'As far as Rosie is concerned, you've got to give me a little more time. Let me speak to her again. Let me see what she says when I tell her we're together.'

Francesca's lips were mutinous. 'And what if she convinces you that I'm the one you shouldn't trust?'

'She won't.'

'You don't know that.'

'Oh, I do.' He was very definite about that. 'You see, the difference is that I don't care what she thinks happened. I know it wasn't you. That's all that really matters.'

CHAPTER FIFTEEN

FRANCESCA woke suddenly, aware that something must have disturbed her, but unable in those first few seconds of consciousness to comprehend what it might have been.

It was still dark outside, she noticed, forcing herself up on her elbows and glancing drowsily about the room. The light from the street lamp outside barely penetrated the curtained windows, and for a moment she had the uneasy feeling that someone was in the room with her. Or in the flat? she pondered, her breath catching in her throat. She strained to hear any sound from the room next door, but all was quiet. She licked her dry lips. Was someone there?

And then her brain cleared. Of course, she thought tremulously, there was someone else in the flat. Will was here; Will, who had turned up the night before and restored her faith in miracles. Will, who had held her, and kissed her, and made love to her; who had convinced her that they were meant to be together.

She expelled the breath she had hardly been aware she was holding, and turned to see the man lying beside her. She just wanted to look at him, she thought—to touch him. To feel his warmth, to burrow down beside him, safe in the knowledge that he loved her—

He wasn't there.

She blinked, not believing it at first. She had been so convinced that it must have been Will who had awakened her, and now she was left with the awful suspicion that she had only dreamed that he had come back for her. Was she only imagining the sweet languor that still gripped her at the memory of his lovemaking? Was that melting sensation inside her just a counterfeit emotion, after all?

A sob caught in her throat.

No!

It wasn't true.

Will had been here.

And, as she lay there, feeling the hot tears burning the backs of her eyes, the conviction that she had not imagined it became a reality. She remembered it so clearly; she couldn't have been dreaming. She remembered his taste, and his smell, the smooth texture of his skin. Remembered how he had felt over her, and under her, his muscled hardness a perfect counterpoint to the softness of her yielding flesh.

She breathed shallowly. Dreams didn't leave you with enumerable aches and pains in unexpected parts of your body, she thought unsteadily. Dreams didn't leave your breasts bruised and tender, or cause a definite soreness between your legs...

A half-laugh escaped her. He had been insatiable, she remembered now. No wonder she ached in places she'd never ached before. Their lovemaking had been by turns slow and tender, fast and furious, and each time he had brought her to a mind-numbing climax she had given away a little more of the defensive shield that had sustained her all those years they were apart. She should have been frightened, but she hadn't been. After what she had suffered before, she should have felt some restraint. But, God help her, she hadn't. She trusted Will. Whatever happened, he was the one steady rock in her life.

So where was he?

Although she had slumped back against the pillows, now she struggled into a sitting position. It crossed her mind that it might have been Will getting out of bed that had disturbed her. When she ran her fingers beneath the quilt, his side of the bed was still warm.

She shivered as the cool air chilled her hot flesh. She

was naked, which was proof, if more was needed, that she had not gone to bed alone. Her nightshirt was still folded under her pillow and she caught her lower lip between her teeth as the recollection of the hours before she had fallen asleep drifted over her again. Oh, God, she thought, she loved him. Loved him so much, it was incredible to think she had survived five whole years without him in her life.

But she didn't want to think about that now. Will was here, and after last night she could have no doubts about his commitment to her. They were going to get married again—as soon as possible, Will had said. He had no intention of running the risk that she might have any excuse for walking out on him again.

Francesca smiled. As if she would. She was even prepared to make an effort to tolerate his grandmother if that was what he wanted. She had Will. She could afford to be generous. She'd never forget, of course, but perhaps she could learn to forgive.

But where was Will?

The sudden explosion of sound from the living room briefly paralysed her.

The flat had been so quiet, and although she'd had no doubt that Will was about somewhere—either in the kitchen or the bathroom, perhaps—the sudden crash, as of bodies falling heavily across her coffee table, petrified her.

What on earth was going on? she wondered numbly, staring towards the door. And then, realising that Will might be in danger, she scrambled hastily out of bed.

There were animal sounds coming from the other room now, and voices, garbled voices, grunting words she couldn't begin to understand. She had made it across the room before she realised she couldn't go out there without any clothes, and, snatching up Will's shirt, which she now saw was lying on the floor at her feet, she pushed her arms into the sleeves and, wrapping it about her, cracked open the door.

At first she couldn't see anything, but the light switch was beside the door and she switched it on.

Instantly, terror gripped her. It was like a scene from some horror movie. Two men—one of them Will—were rolling about the floor and at first glance there seemed to be blood everywhere. The second man had a knife, and Will was trying desperately to get it away from him, and the blood came from the numerous cuts and grazes she could see on his skin. Apart from anything else, the fact that Will was only wearing his shorts obviously gave his opponent the advantage, and Francesca clenched her fists and gazed helplessly about her, wishing there were something she could do.

Even as she watched, the other man succeeded in delivering a crippling punch to Will's head. She felt the blow herself, the sickening crack as the man's fist connected with Will's temple causing a sympathetic pain in her own skull. The man was bigger, and heavier, and obviously violent. A black-clad figure, wearing black gloves, his face disguised behind a black Balaclava.

A *Balaclava*!

Francesca's knees turned to jelly beneath her. She had no need to wonder who the intruder was any longer, or why he had chosen to break into her apartment. She knew him as surely as if he had rung a bell and announced his arrival. This was the man who had been stalking her for the past six months. Not Tom Radley, or that pathetic creature who'd admitted to the offence, but this man. And somehow Will had heard him—had apprehended him before he could get to her.

She caught her breath. She had to do something, and do it quickly. If only there were a phone in the bedroom, but there wasn't. The only phone in the flat was in the living room, and their heaving bodies were between her and it.

She groaned. If anything happened to Will, she'd never forgive herself. This was her mess, not his, and she couldn't just stand there watching that pervert cut him to pieces. If only she had a weapon...

An awful choking sound brought her eyes back to the two men on the floor. Somehow—she wasn't sure how—Will had managed to get out from under the other man, and now he had him in a grinding headlock. It was the pressure he was exerting on the man's throat that was causing him to make those awful guttural sounds, and she was sure Will intended to break his neck.

Her lips parted to make a protest, to implore Will not to kill the man and thus destroy his own life as well, when Will saw her.

An expression of raw frustration crossed his face at that moment, and perhaps his momentary lapse of concentration caused him to loosen his hold. And, obviously sensing Will's distraction, the other man took the opportunity to fill his lungs with air, and brought his elbow back into Will's stomach with all the force he could muster.

Will gasped, unable to breathe for a few seconds, and when his arms went limp the other man sprang free. He was facing Will now, balanced on the soles of his feet, in a half-crouching posture, poised to strike again, the knife-blade glistening in the light.

'No!'

Without a thought for her own safety, Francesca dived across the room, vaulting onto the man's back and winding her arms and legs about him. Her hands groped instinctively for his face, finding the eyeholes in the Balaclava, and without hesitation she dug her fingers into his eyes.

The man grunted in agony, all his attention turned to getting her off his back. And Will recovered himself sufficiently to grab his wrist and wrestle the knife from him. Staggering slightly, he gripped the knife in his hand, but Francesca guessed he'd lost a lot of blood. There were cuts all over his arms and legs, and one particularly nasty-looking tear in the flesh of his side.

Still, he had the knife now, and although he might look battle-scarred she didn't think anyone would be foolish enough to try and take it away from him. There was a look of such savage determination on his lean, good-looking face, she hardly recognised him herself.

Meanwhile, the man was attempting to fling her off his back, but Francesca had one more thing she wanted to do. As he groped blindly to dislodge her, she grasped a handful of coarse wool and tore off the concealing Balaclava.

Beneath the helmet, the man's head was closely cropped, his neck stocky, his bunchy shoulders those of a rugby forward. Catching her breath in wonder, Francesca dropped nervelessly from his shoulders, and circled him with disbelieving eyes.

'Mick!' she exclaimed incredulously, staring at him as if she couldn't believe her eyes. 'Oh, my God! *Mick!*'

'You know him?'

Will was still breathing heavily, and Francesca nodded. 'It's Mick,' she said dully. 'Mick Callaghan. Clare's husband.'

It was later, much later, after the police had taken Mick away, and Will had returned from the hospital, after having his wounds attended to, that he remembered about the note he'd found in her letterbox.

He was stiff, very stiff, but he managed to pull the scrap of paper out of his pocket and show it to her, the three words it contained cut out of a newspaper or a magazine.

'"There's no escape,"' read Francesca slowly, her pale cheeks an indication of how she would have felt if she'd found the note. She licked her lips and looked at him. 'Then you knew he was still out there. Was that why you insisted on spending the night?'

'Oh, sure.' Will was half sitting, half reclining on the sofa, while Francesca was perched on the arm beside him, and now he looked up at her with weary eyes. 'Has what I said meant nothing? Do you still have doubts about my motives? For God's sake, Fran, that's like hitting a man while he's down.'

Francesca winced. 'Do you mean that?'

'Of course I mean it.' Will closed his eyes for a moment, not sure he had the strength to convince her of anything tonight. 'In any case, as far as I was concerned, the man was behind bars.'

'Oh, yes.'

Her lips parted, and Will, opening his eyes again, wished he could just crawl into her bed. They'd given him some medication at the hospital, to ease the pain of his cuts and bruises, and he was woozy. He badly wanted somewhere to lay his head.

'But you were up,' she pointed out now, and he sighed.

'It preyed on my mind,' he admitted. 'But that's not why I was out of bed. I thought I'd heard something. Perhaps it was when he opened the door. I'm used to the quiet of Lingard. Any sound was strange to me.'

'Thank God for that!'

'Yes.' Will nodded. 'Luckily, he was still in the foyer when I slipped out of the bedroom. I guess he thought you'd be in bed. Alone.'

Francesca shivered. 'It's frightening to think of what might have happened if you hadn't been here.'

'Hmm.' Will met her gaze with steady eyes. 'I guess I'm more territorial than I thought. If he'd hurt you, I'd have killed him. I never knew I had that in me. When I saw you standing in the doorway, I'd never felt so helpless in my life.'

'But you must have known I was there. I turned on the lights.'

'I guess I was too busy at that moment to pay any attention to it,' said Will feelingly. 'My head was buzzing. Callaghan packs quite a punch, you know.'

Francesca slid down onto the sofa beside him. 'I almost ruined everything, didn't I?' she said, smoothing soft fingers across his brow. And although Will was tired his body stirred automatically and, capturing her hand in his, he brought it to his lips.

'You were great,' he said huskily. 'Though I guess it was my fault that you hadn't bolted the door.'

'Oh, yes.' Francesca nestled closer. 'You told the police he'd used a key to get in.' She moaned. 'Oh, God, I left my spare set of keys with Clare that weekend I was away.'

'And he must have had a copy made,' remarked Will heavily, his hand curving possessively round her thigh. 'Callaghan probably didn't know you normally used a bolt as well. When he tried the key and it worked, he must have thought he was home and dry.'

'So you don't think he broke the window before?'

'No. Breaking windows isn't Callaghan's style. As you said, he liked to follow you, to make you feel uneasy, so he possibly knew the window was broken anyway. The guy who confessed probably had tried to break in, like he said.'

Francesca looked up at him. 'What do you think he intended to do?' She paused. 'Mick, I mean.'

'I don't know. Scare you, terrify you. Make you think you weren't safe anywhere.'

'You don't think—' Francesca hesitated. 'You don't think he would have raped me?'

Will's tone was harsh. 'Thank God we'll never know.'

Francesca nodded. 'Poor Clare,' she said feelingly, imagining how her friend was going to feel when she found out. 'He was playing such a—a stupid game. I—I could have recognised him. I would have, if he'd ever got that close.'

'But would you have reported him?' asked Will grimly. 'Knowing what it would do to Clare if you did?'

Francesca shook her head. 'She'd never have believed me.'

'But she would have had her doubts,' said Will quietly. 'These people destroy their family's lives as well as their own.'

'Oh, poor Clare.'

Francesca was looking distraught now, and, realising he couldn't let her go to sleep on that note, Will curled one hand behind her head and brought her mouth to his.

Immediately, the heat of their passion was rekindled again, burning away the pain of treachery and betrayal. Despite his injuries, Will was not immune to the eager pressure of her lips beneath his, and it was only when she pressed him back against the cushions that he let out an involuntary groan.

'What is it? What's the matter?'

Francesca was all contrition, and with an effort Will forced a reassuring grin. 'It's nothing,' he said. 'I'm just a bit tender around my midriff, that's all.'

'Oh, God! Your stitches!' she protested, obviously recalling the treatment he had had at the hospital. 'I'm sorry.' And, unbuttoning his shirt, she bent and laid her lips against the bandage that the doctor had secured around his middle. 'Let's go to bed.'

'I thought you'd never ask,' said Will weakly, and Francesca lifted her head and bestowed a warm kiss at the corner of his mouth.

'I love you,' she breathed, saying the only words he really wanted to hear. 'And no one—particularly not your grandmother—is going to keep us apart.'

CHAPTER SIXTEEN

THE letter came about two weeks after Will had brought Francesca back to live at the Abbey.

It was two months since Will had caught Clare's husband breaking into the flat, and although Mick had denied being the man who had terrorised her for so many months the crime he had committed, and for which he would be convicted, was sufficiently serious to ensure that he'd probably spend the next several years in prison.

And his arrest had explained so many things, not least why Francesca had had no phone calls the weekend she was away in Yorkshire. He had also known about the other man's arrest and confession, and had probably decided to wait and give Francesca a false sense of her own security. It also explained how the stalker had known her new phone number. Naturally, she had given her new number to Clare, and it had been a simple matter for Mick to find out what it was.

Clare herself had come to see Francesca to apologise for what she saw as her part in what had happened. She'd been upset, of course, but, contrary to Francesca's fears, she hadn't blamed her friend for what Mick had done. Since he'd lost his job, he'd changed, she'd said. And she'd always known he was attracted to Francesca, even though he had never said as much to her. She still loved him, she'd insisted, but she would assist the police as much as she could. Mick needed help, and the kindest thing she could do was to ensure that he got it.

For her part, now that she and Will were together again, Francesca had been quite happy to give in her notice at Teniko, and explain to Mrs Bernstein that she'd be leaving the flat. She had had to work her notice, of course, and Will had had to return to Yorkshire in the meantime, but they had spoken every night on the phone, and at weekends Will had driven the two hundred or so miles to spend Saturday and Sunday with her.

It had been a period of adjustment for both of them, but they were both glad when it was over. By mutual agreement, they had decided not to tell anyone that they were getting back together until Francesca was able to leave London, and it had been doubly hard for Will, balancing what he told his grandmother with what he was actually doing.

Whether she had had an inkling of what was going on Francesca didn't know, but on the morning they'd presented themselves at Mulberry Court the old woman had regarded them both with equal disgust.

'I always knew you couldn't be trusted,' she said to Francesca coldly, and when Will protested she turned on him in obvious frustration.

'You don't care, do you?' she accused him. 'You don't care what happens to Lingard, so long as you have this woman in your bed! Well, one day you'll understand all I've done for you, and for Lingard, and you'll be sorry.'

'I doubt it, old lady,' said Will, with maddening civility. 'I love Fran. I always have. And that means more to me than a pile of bricks and mortar.'

'Lingard is not a pile of bricks and mortar!' exclaimed his grandmother fiercely. 'It's my—*your* heritage. And without an infusion of capital—real capital, such as the Merritts would have provided—it has no chance of surviving into the next century.'

Will sighed. 'And that's why you drove Fran away, is it? Because she didn't have any money?'

'Fran!' Lady Rosemary gave the young woman in question a contemptuous look. 'I didn't send her away, Will. She walked out, remember? When you found out she'd got rid of an unwelcome pregnancy.'

Francesca gasped. 'That's not true. You know that's not true.'

'Do I?' Will's grandmother was scathing. 'All I know is, my great-grandchild was aborted. Aborted, Will. Never forget that. Oh, she may have other children, if you're lucky, but you'll always remember that what would have been your first-born was terminated against your will—'

'Shut up!'

For a moment, Francesca thought it was she who had said those words. She had certainly wanted to say them. But it was Will who had actually voiced them, his hand gripping her wrist with almost painful intensity as he urged her towards the door.

'I never want to hear you use those words again,' he added, looking down at Francesca. 'If you want to see me—to see either of us—again you'll apologise to my wife for ever doubting her word.'

'Never!'

Lady Rosemary was adamant, and Will jerked open the door, startling Mrs Baxter, who had been about to knock and ask if they'd like any refreshments. 'I suggest you have a few words with Archie Rossiter,' he added, as a parting shot. 'I think you'll find he's the one who's been lying. Not my wife.'

And now, a few days later, a letter had arrived addressed to Lord and Lady Lingard. It was a little premature, thought Francesca ruefully. She and Will had not yet re-tied the marriage knot, and although she wanted to believe it was good news the fact that it had a solicitor's name on the back of the envelope made her nervous.

What now? she thought anxiously, pausing in the doorway to the library, looking across at Will, who was going through the Abbey's accounts with Maurice Fielding, the estate bailiff. They had spent the morning poring over the books, and although it had been a good year it was autumn now, and the gardens would soon be closed to visitors until the spring.

Money was tight; she knew that. And she had every intention of getting a job herself, and playing her part. But the thing was, she was almost sure she was pregnant again, and she wanted to do nothing to jeopardise either the baby's health or the dearly cherished relationship she now had with Will.

She hadn't told him about the baby yet. Although she knew he would be delighted, she didn't want to put any further burden on his shoulders until she was absolutely sure. She would have liked to have hidden this letter, too. But Mrs Harvey had handed it to her, so she had to show it to Will.

She drew a breath, and, ever vigilant of his wife's presence, Will looked up and gave her a lazy smile. He stretched then, arching his back luxuriously, and Francesca knew what he was thinking when his eyes rested on her slender form.

'This came,' she said awkwardly, gesturing with the envelope, and Maurice Fielding got immediately to his feet.

'Well, it's lunchtime,' he said, with remarkable tact, and pushed his arms into the sleeves of the jacket which he'd draped over the back of his chair. 'You're looking well, madam, if I may say so?' He glanced round at Will. 'D'you want to continue this after lunch, my lord?'

'Tomorrow, I think,' said Will, his eyes still on Francesca, and then, getting up, too, he indicated that she should come in. He came round the desk and slung an arm across her slim shoulders. 'See you in the morning, Maurice. About ten, okay?'

Fielding nodded, and with another shy look in Francesca's direction he went out of the room and closed the door. Will barely waited until the door had closed before he bent his head and kissed her, his hands in the loosened glory of her hair, his tongue plunging deeply into her mouth.

'Will!'

When she could speak, Francesca offered the half-hearted protest. She hadn't yet got used to Will's predilection for making love to her when and where he pleased. It wasn't that she didn't like it; it was just that she was more self-conscious than he was. But she couldn't deny how delightful it made her feel.

'I love you,' he said, nuzzling her neck, and she wished she could just ignore the letter as he was evidently able to do. At times like these, the usual outcome was a prolonged lunch break in their room, with food coming very low on their list of priorities.

'I think you should look at this letter,' she murmured unhappily, her hands on his forearms gently urging him away. 'It looks very official. Do you think it's from your grandmother?' She hesitated. 'There's nothing she can do to spoil things, is there?'

'I shouldn't think so.' Will let her go reluctantly, and took the envelope from her hand. 'Lingard is mine. Nothing she can do can change that. And this house is what she cares about, after all.'

'Oh, I think she cares about you, too,' said Francesca ruefully, unable to be anything but honest. 'She's just—disappointed in your choice of wife.'

'Her loss,' said Will drily, slitting the envelope open. He frowned. 'It's from her solicitors: Wright and Peel.'

'They are her solicitors, then.' Francesca's heart sank. 'What do they say?'

There were actually two letters, she saw as Will pulled them out. One evidently from the solicitors, the other in a sealed envelope that Will opened after scanning the first. Then he read them both again, his expression darkening as he did so, and Francesca's spirits sank into her shoes. It could only be bad news for him to look so grave.

'They're not from the old lady,' Will said at last, in a low voice. 'Wright and Peel are her solicitors, but apparently they're Archie Rossiter's solicitors, too.' He heaved a sigh, and thrust them towards her. 'Here. You'd better read what he's written.'

Francesca would have much rather that he had told her. All she could think was that Lady Rosemary had thought of something else to tear them apart. Only this time she'd enlisted Dr Rossiter's assistance. She probably thought his evidence had proved crucial before.

The letter from the solicitors was straightforward enough. They merely stated that they had been asked by their client, Mr Archibald Rossiter, to forward this communication to them. They added that they had also taken a written statement from Mr Rossiter, which he had asked them to keep in their files. Should either Will or herself wish to use that statement, the solicitors had Mr Rossiter's permission to hand it to them at that time.

Francesca blinked, and lifted her head to give Will a puzzled look, but he was standing staring bleakly out of the window, his face set and remote. Dear God, she thought, what had the old man written? What could he have said that he hadn't said already?

Her hand trembling, she lifted the second letter. This time, instead of their official appellation, the letter was addressed to Will and Francesca. She tried not to feel any optimism at this informal styling, and as Will still wasn't looking at her she began to read.

My dear Will and Francesca,
I have wanted for so long to write this letter, but while my late wife was alive, I am ashamed to say I felt compelled to keep my guilt from her. She was a sick woman for several years before providence put an end to her pain, and I could not have added to her suffering by revealing what I had done.

Your grandmother is a most persuasive woman, Will, but I firmly believe that in other circumstances I would not have given in to her pleas. But, as I have said, Lavinia was ill; she was in desperate need of an operation, and unfortunately her treatment could only be found overseas at that time. In return for services rendered, your grandmother paid for Lavinia and me to travel to the United States for that treatment. I was only a working general practitioner. My salary did not run to expensive trips abroad, with all expenses paid. Lady Rosemary paid for everything, and, I have to say, gave Lavinia a few more months of life.

You will have guessed what my role was to be. Will, your grandmother convinced me that Francesca did not want that child, otherwise I would never have terminated her pregnancy. Afterwards, of course, it was too late to regret it, and Lady Rosemary got her way: your marriage ended.

Since Lavinia's death, I've been tempted to tell you the truth so many times, but I was sure it was too late to put matters right. Then, a few days ago, when your grandmother came to tell me you were getting back together, I knew I had been given a second chance.

Needless to say, your grandmother does not know about this letter, nor about the sworn statement I have lodged with Wright and Peel. It's yours, to do with as you will. With Lavinia gone, I have nothing to lose.

One final point. It's a lot to ask, I know, but I would beg your forgiveness. However you choose to use my statement, that would mean more to me than anything else.

The gasp Francesca gave as she finished reading the letter at last forced Will to turn his head and look at her. But his eyes were dark, his expression strained and disbelieving, and she guessed what the old doctor's confession must mean to him.

'You've read it,' he said flatly, and although Francesca could understand his feelings she was chilled by the lack of emotion in his face.

'Yes,' she said. And then, with a slightly uncertain smile, she added, 'Vindication at last.'

'Is that how you see it? Vindication?' Will expelled

a short breath. 'God—I can't believe she'd do such a thing!'

'No.' Francesca bent her head, unwilling to labour the point that she knew that already. 'I—suppose she had her reasons. Or she thought she had anyway.'

Will shook his head. 'I'll never forgive her. Never!'

Francesca caught her breath. 'You have to.'

'Why?' His lips twisted. 'Because old Rossiter has confessed? Fran, it was my grandmother who ordered his actions, who used the old man's love for his wife to further her own ends.'

Francesca heaved an unsteady breath. 'I know.'

'So.' Will was harsh. 'What are you going to do about it? You'll have to get yourself another solicitor. It would be a conflict of interests if Wright and Peel—'

'Will!' Francesca covered the space he'd opened between them, and put a tentative hand on his sleeve. 'Will, I'm not going to do anything. What could I do? I've got nothing to gain now.'

'Just your innocence,' said Will bitterly, covering her hand with his for a moment, and then, as if it was too painful for him to touch her, he pulled his hand away. 'I'd want some retribution if I were you. God, if I hadn't been so stupid, I'd want it for myself.'

Francesca took hold of his hand and brought it back to where it had briefly rested. 'I don't need that,' she assured him softly. 'All right. I know you didn't believe your grandmother disliked me that much, but I've always known. I confronted her that day she came to the Abbey when you were out. She wouldn't admit it, but she knew I knew she was lying. Only we both thought you would never believe me then. Now you do, and that's all that matters. We don't need the old man's testimony to prove our love.'

Will groaned. 'You're not saying you can forgive me? Not after the way I've treated you.'

Francesca linked her arms about his neck. 'My dar-

ling, I forgave you years ago. I just never believed I'd
be able to convince you to take me back.'

Will's arms closed about her, and all the emotion she
had thought was missing from his expression returned
with passionate force. 'Oh, God,' he said, burying his
face in her neck. 'I was sure Archie's confession would
drive a wedge between us again.'

'No chance,' said Francesca huskily. 'We've got too
much on our side.

It was early evening when the news came from Mulberry
Court. Lady Rosemary had had a stroke, and had been
rushed into hospital.

'It was just after Dr Rossiter left,' Mrs Baxter told
Will, rather tearfully. 'I phoned for an ambulance immediately. It's St Margaret's. I expect you'll want to go.'

'You must go,' said Francesca, when he broke the
news to her. 'You'll never forgive yourself if you don't
go and see her. She is your grandmother, after all.'

It was almost midnight when he got back. His face
was drawn, but it brightened considerably when he saw
Francesca. Hugging her close, he told her Lady
Rosemary had died an hour ago, but not before she had
admitted to Will her part in trying to break him and
Francesca up.

Neither of them said as much, but they both suspected
that Archie Rossiter had been partially responsible for
the stroke she had suffered. He must have told her what
he'd done that evening, and it had been too much for
her to take. She was an old woman, after all. And she
had lived a full life. In many ways, it was better for her
that it should have ended this way.

'I didn't mention the letter,' Will confessed some time
later, after he and Francesca were in bed. He gathered
her closer. 'I think she hoped I'd think she'd had a
change of heart. In any event she told me she hoped
we'd be happy now that I knew the truth.'

Francesca's lips twitched. 'She wanted the last word,' she said softly, and Will nodded.

'I think so.'

She sighed. 'If only she could have swallowed her pride and accepted the status quo all those years ago.' She bit her lip. 'Our child would have been almost five years old now.'

Will pressed his face into her neck. 'We'll have others.'

Francesca nodded. 'I hope so.' She darted a glance up at him. 'If we can afford them, of course.'

'Oh—' Will grimaced '—we'll manage.'

'That's good.' Francesca dimpled. 'Because there is something you should know...'

The final chapter of the story was written some ten days later. Lady Rosemary's funeral was a rather grand affair, with dignitaries coming from as far away as London and the Continent to pay their last respects. Archie Rossiter was there, of course, and he took the opportunity to have a word with Will and Francesca after it was all over. He confessed that although he'd gone to Mulberry Court to tell Lady Rosemary what he'd done he'd not found the courage to do so.

'I'm glad now, of course,' he said as Will and Francesca looked at one another. 'Though I suppose you now have no proof to confirm what I said.'

'Oh, we have,' said Will drily, unable to condemn the old man to an anxious grave. 'My grandmother admitted that she'd asked you to—end the pregnancy when I went to the hospital the night she had the stroke.'

'Thank heaven!' said the old man gratefully. 'You've restored my faith in human nature.'

He didn't ask what they were going to do about his confession. Will told Francesca he'd ask the solicitors to destroy the statement after the reading of his grandmother's will. And in that will they had another surprise waiting for them. Lady Rosemary had left her jewels in trust to her grandson's wife.

'To do with as she thinks fit,' intoned the solicitor, and Francesca caught her breath.

'The old—devil,' she said, squeezing Will's arm. 'She was determined you would have the money to restore the Abbey, after all.'

FIVE STARS
MEAN SUCCESS

If you see the "5 Star Club" flash on a book,
it means we're introducing you to one of our
most STELLAR authors!

Every one of our Harlequin and Silhouette
authors who has sold over 5 MILLION BOOKS
has been selected for our "5 Star Club."

We've created the club so you won't miss
any of our bestsellers. So, each month
we'll be highlighting every original book within
Harlequin and Silhouette written by our
bestselling authors.

NOW THERE'S NO WAY ON EARTH OUR STARS WON'T BE SEEN!

5 STAR CLUB
AUTHOR

 HARLEQUIN®    Silhouette®

P5STAR

HARLEQUIN ULTIMATE GUIDES™

A series of how-to books for today's woman.

Act now to order some of these extremely
helpful guides just for you!

*Whatever the situation, Harlequin Ultimate Guides™
has all the answers!*

#80507	HOW TO TALK TO A	$4.99 U.S. ☐
	NAKED MAN	$5.50 CAN.☐
#80508	I CAN FIX THAT	$5.99 U.S. ☐
		$6.99 CAN.☐
#80510	WHAT YOUR TRAVEL AGENT	$5.99 U.S. ☐
	KNOWS THAT YOU DON'T	$6.99 CAN.☐
#80511	RISING TO THE OCCASION	
	More Than Manners: Real Life	$5.99 U.S. ☐
	Etiquette for Today's Woman	$6.99 CAN.☐
#80513	WHAT GREAT CHEFS	$5.99 U.S. ☐
	KNOW THAT YOU DON'T	$6.99 CAN.☐
#80514	WHAT SAVVY INVESTORS	$5.99 U.S. ☐
	KNOW THAT YOU DON'T	$6.99 CAN.☐
#80509	GET WHAT YOU WANT OUT OF	$5.99 U.S. ☐
	LIFE—AND KEEP IT!	$6.99 CAN.☐

(quantities may be limited on some titles)

TOTAL AMOUNT	$
POSTAGE & HANDLING	$
(\$1.00 for one book, 50¢ for each additional)	
APPLICABLE TAXES*	$ _____
TOTAL PAYABLE	$ _____

(check or money order—please do not send cash)

To order, complete this form and send it, along with a check or money
order for the total above, payable to Harlequin Ultimate Guides, to:
In the U.S.: 3010 Walden Avenue, P.O. Box 9047, Buffalo, NY
14269-9047; **In Canada:** P.O. Box 613, Fort Erie, Ontario, L2A 5X3.

Name: _____

Address: _____ City: _____

State/Prov.: _____ Zip/Postal Code: _____

*New York residents remit applicable sales taxes.
Canadian residents remit applicable GST and provincial taxes.

◆ HARLEQUIN®

Look us up on-line at: http://www.romance.net

HNF8L4

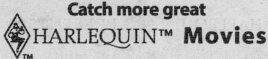

 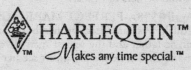

HARLEQUIN PRESENTS®

Introduces a brand-new miniseries from

The Crightons are a family that appears to have everything—money, position, power and elegance, but one fateful weekend threatens to destroy it all!

March 1998—THE PERFECT SEDUCTION (#1941)
The Crighton family had been the cause of scandal and heartache for Bobbie Miller, and she wanted revenge. All she had to do was seduce Luke Crighton, and the family secrets would be hers to expose.

April 1998—PERFECT MARRIAGE MATERIAL (#1948)
Tullah was tantalized by her boss, Saul Crighton. A devoted single father and the sexiest man alive, he was perfect marriage material. But he plainly didn't see her as the perfect wife!

May 1998—THE PERFECT MATCH? (#1954)
When Chrissie met Guy, she thought her most romantic fantasies had just come to life. But Chrissie had a family secret that Guy could surely never forgive....

Available wherever Harlequin books are sold.

HPPJPF